Getting Away With MURDER

Pele Plante

Clothespin Fever Press
Los Angeles 1991

Dedication:
To Anne, with love and appreciation

Acknowledgements:
Heartfelt thanks to my writers' group, especially Margo and Suzanne for their critiques. Much appreciation also to Paula, Julie and Mary, dear friends offering encouragement at just the right times, as did daughter Erin, too. And special thanks to Jenny Wrenn, a superb editor.

Clothespin Fever Press
5529 N. Figueroa, Los Angeles, CA 90042

First Edition

All the characters and organizations in this book are fictitious and any resemblance to persons living or dead is purely coincidental.

Cataloging information:

Plante, Pele.
Getting away with murder.

1. Title
813.54

ISBN:1-878533-00-2

Chapter 1

A rifle shot ricocheted off the hills behind the house. Blakely Lancaster, our deputy sheriff, leaped out of the kitchen chair and ran for the terrace, pulling his revolver out of its holster as he went.

Despite his gesture to stay behind, Barb and I followed, grabbing binoculars on the way. The neighborhood bird population was also disturbed. A colony of magpies fluttered up into the air and the finches retreated into a thicket, chattering to themselves.

"Be careful, CC. Don't go out in the open," Barbara said.

CC stands for Cynthia Chenery Scott, a name my father imposed on me that never took. Too fussy and frilly for a tomboy.

"Nut thinks he's Daniel Boone." I scanned the hills with the high-powered glasses. The sky was cloudy with some rain expected, providing soft-focus lighting.

Blakely kept racing up the hill, darting from rock

outcropping to the cover of scrub oaks in a zig zag. His tan uniform blended into the golden grass of August.

He had just been explaining, "Still trying to track him down," around lusty mouthfuls of Barbara's apple strudel. We were not above plying him with home-baked goodies to keep abreast of the police news that didn't make the local paper.

It was yet another way of not minding my own business. Sometimes I have fooled myself into believing that attending to someone else's troubles relieved my own. But other people's problems just always looked more interesting than my own, which is no doubt one of the reasons I wound up being a therapist.

"A patient, perhaps." I wondered if the sniper was someone from our local hospital for the mentally ill, a major employer in the county.

"Could be," Barbara replied but her tone was skeptical.

Discharged patients were supposed to return to the geographical area of their origin, but patients wanted to stay close to the hospital, clinging to its security, a tenuous handhold on the ladder of reality.

"Blakely thinks an old-timer could have gotten fed up with the newcomers moving in here and might be trying to scare them off."

"Either way, not too balanced," I observed. "Might just as easily take a potshot at a human."

"Look at what I have, girls." Kathryn appeared at the fence between our acreages. She carried a small cardboard box. In it was an American goldfinch, looking quite dead lying on its back with feet up in the air.

"It's not dead." Barbara indicated a pulse in its throat.

"I know, just stunned," Kathryn agreed. "It will come around. It flew into my window."

"I thought for a minute that it had something to do with that rifle shot." I was relieved the sniper hadn't shot down into our yards.

"No. But I knew you'd both be out here when you heard the shot, and I wanted to show you the goldfinch."

"He's beautiful." I touched his glossy black cap gently, stroking the little creature to reassure it.

"This is my magic box," Kathryn went on. "Put an injured bird in here and even if it takes hours, they revive."

"Yes, the experts say a quiet dark place is what is needed for recovery." I could have added, just as for humans.

"Phil was annoyed with me for saving birds. Said they would just eat his fruit." Her expression was sentimental.

"It is a difficult choice, whether to have wildlife or agriculture." Barb smiled at her.

"Are they going to catch that nut, or what?" Kathryn knew of our cultivation of Blakely. A former city cop who had sickened of the crack babies and gang violence, he relished the peaceableness of this quiet county.

Blakely returned, out of breath and annoyed.

"He must live in a nearby house. Just goes back into his hole."

"Can you get a search warrant?" I thought they better put a stop to it before someone actually got shot.

"Not in America." Blakely grinned.

"People have a right to bear arms," Kathryn spoke up.

"We'll catch up with him," Blakely promised. "Or her."

He tended to mind his pronouns around us.

The sniper was shrewd, executing these random blasts every few weeks. Just when the Lucca Valley was lulled into thinking it was over another would shatter the stillness. They had begun the first day of the hunting season. We thought it was just accidental at first. Some hunter cleaning a gun.

After the third time it happened, calls lit up the sheriff's switchboard like a Christmas tree. As the only deputies patrolling the entire north county, Blakely and his relief, Theresa Madera, were hard pressed to apprehend the suspect.

No one had been shot, no shells had been found, leading Blakely and Theresa to believe the sniper was not firing live ammunition, just terrorizing the neighborhood with blanks.

A reward for information had been offered through the Crimewatchers' fund, but nothing had proved to be a viable lead.

Blakely polished off his strudel and accepted another cup of coffee. "Maybe I should set up surveillance here. This would be a good spot to keep a watch for the sniper 'cause you can see most of the hill from here. We could all take turns."

I started to agree, but stopped cold at Barbara's look.

He shrugged. Close cropped red hair with flecks of frosted blonde framed green-gray eyes. A stubborn jaw contradicted his soft voice. He finished his coffee.

"Better go call in," he muttered and left.

"Hope he doesn't get in trouble." Barbara looked worried.

"Why?" I didn't see what was wrong.

"He didn't use proper police procedure. He should have called in for backup first and then gone out to investigate."

"But that nut isn't going to wait for protocol!"

Barbara smiled. "The therapist is resorting to the vernacular."

"Not wrapped too tight. Only one oar in the water," I teased irreverently.

Chapter 2

"I think he's after her property, CC."

Jennifer had dropped over for a private consultation and was sitting on the end of my kitchen counter, her feet dangling and fidgeting in their cute black booties, while I made my favorite marmalade.

"What makes you think that?" I kept slivering orange peel.

"Auntie had all of her mortgage papers out, showing them to him."

"Maybe he was giving her financial advice." If it were a romantic interest, it was too soon. Phil had been dead only three months.

"Auntie!" Jennifer snorted. "She is a financial wizard. Better than Uncle Phil."

"Maybe she was advising him." I still didn't see anything wrong.

"I read a brochure he left for her."

At my raised eyebrow, she had the grace to blush. It was easy for me to see when someone else was meddling.

"While Auntie was in the bathroom," she admitted.

"What did it say?"

"His foundation takes title to the property and makes the mortgage payments. She lives rent free for the rest of her life." Jennifer helped herself to some more coffee.

"A kind of reverse mortgage?" I asked as I put the citrus in a pan to soak with a teaspoon of baking powder.

"Not exactly. She doesn't get any equity payments or money out of the deal."

Jennifer was an artist. She marketed her soft sculptures with sharp business sense, although you'd never know it to look at her spiked hair and wild clothes. Today a purple tunic and black leggings. A lot like my own beatnik days. Black turtleneck sweaters, coffeehouse folk music, wild poetry readings...oops, stay out of the past; pay attention to the present. That was what I was always telling clients.

"What about repairs and maintenance?"

"His agency, Shelterworks, takes care of everything. It's a place for the homeless."

"Sounds too good to be true. There must be a catch."

"The catch is you have to be over seventy and screened by Jeffrey Randall."

"Over seventies don't have a long life span." I said, acutely aware of this myself, the older I got. At mid-fifty, seventy didn't look so far away.

"Which is why the whole thing stinks," Jennifer went on. "He's taking advantage of old people."

"There must be some legal recourse?"

"I checked it out. The district attorney says there is nothing we can do about it. It's a living trust. Perfectly legal," she said as she put her cup down hard on the counter.

"Oh, really?" I was hooked and took my cue. "We'll just keep an eye on things. See if we can find out any more about this fellow. Maybe he's not so slick after all. Maybe he'll slip up somewhere."

"You will? That's wonderful." Jennifer slipped off the counter to hug me. "I was afraid you would say there was nothing to it. Jake, you know how he is, says it sounds like a good deal. He's so naive he doesn't realize we are Auntie's heirs."

"I can see the reason for your concern."

"I can't be here as much as I would like because of the demonstrations, so it really means a lot to me that you are such good neighbors to Auntie."

"I understand."

Jennifer lived nearby at Buena Beach, where there was a lot of protest activity against offshore oil drilling. Sometimes we'd see her on the six o'clock news, riding out to sea in a tiny skiff with other activists to disrupt the seismic survey ships. Their sonic soundings were destroying the ecology of the ocean floor, a nursery for marine life.

All my life I had missed the call of civil disobedience. When the free speech movement turned into a blossoming of civil rights for blacks and women, I was doing my internship, trying to deal with the aftermath of human misery from Viet Nam. It was all I could handle.

I had experienced a calling of sorts to do what I could to relieve human suffering as a therapist. But I followed the evening news of the peace movement hungrily, all too aware that it was doing just fine without me.

Settling into a rhythm of work, setting up serious housekeeping with Barbara and buying our first home, all served to keep me quite busy in our own backyard.

When the women's movement torpedoed into the seventies, I supported it, too. In fact, CR (consciousness raising) groups asked me to speak to them about alternative lifestyles (the CR rap for lesbians). But it felt like they were just catching up with us. Also, I was uneasy with some who seemed to be choosing to love women because it was politically incorrect to love men. Political lesbians, we called them.

However, I followed the lead players, bought the music and the books, and even attended a women's retreat, but never really was part of the action.

With the building of a nuclear power plant at Buena Beach, again I missed the boat, letting the younger generation do my demonstrating and protesting for me, unwilling to risk not being there for my clients if I couldn't be bailed out easily, or was injured.

To tell the truth, I was just plain scared. Watching young students get set on with police dogs and fire

taught junior high.

Barbara was squinting behind her binoculars, watching the vultures, five huge black birds with blood-red faces, twisting and pulling at a deer carcass. The animal lay in the grass under a barbed wire fence, in the upper pasture. The position of the dead deer revealed what must have happened. While jumping the fence, a hoof caught on the top strand, bringing the big blacktail down. A rock lay beside its head.

"At least it didn't suffer," she murmured, adjusting her glasses to get a sharper picture, and then passing them to me.

"Look how the tips of their wings are separated like fingers. Helps keep them aloft when they're soaring," she explained.

I looked at her, always in awe of her storehouse of information. Survival ploys leftover from teaching in the city when she needed to throw out morsels to keep her savage students' attention.

Barbara Bettencourt was tall and muscular. An amazon, I called her. She wore her straight black hair in an avant garde haircut with the back shorter than the sides, curving over her high cheekbones. Nice to look at.

Five deer shared the land with us. We advocated peaceful co-existence, but the deer were cheeky and irritated us by nibbling our roses and lettuces. However vexed we got at them, though, the sight of such wild grace bounding about stirred us. We'd have to stop whatever we were doing and watch.

The deer have been in residence in North America tens of thousands of years before our kind, Barbara had said, explaining how intertwined our history was with that of the deer.

But it was the vultures who held center stage today.

"Seems to be a pecking order." Barbara indicated a new arrival to whom the other birds deferred. When one of the feeding vultures didn't move away from the carcass soon enough, the newcomer rushed towards the bird with deadly menace.

"What are you girls doing?" Kathryn peered over the fence. Only an elder could get away with calling us girls. An elder who, although small-framed and slight, held herself proudly erect, creating the illusion of a larger presence.

I indicated the deer and vultures up in the pasture and brought my binoculars to Kathryn.

We set up a command post in the backyard with tripods for power scope and camera. The terrace soon was host to a flock of long-legged steel birds. Bird watching, even ghoulish vultures, was a favored avocation.

"What is it?" she asked as I passed her the binoculars. Kathryn was keenly alert. Here was something unusual.

"Vultures feeding on a dead deer," I answered.

"What a shame. Young buck, was it? Looks like a spike." She was as interested as we were.

"Would you like to come over and look through our scope?" Barbara offered.

"No, but thank you. I've promised Jeffrey I would help with a slide show at the center. On wildflowers," she said, her face beaming.

I looked at Barbara in alarm. Phil was dead only three months and here's Kathryn, giddy as a teenager. No wonder Jennifer was concerned about this situation.

"Who is Jeffrey?" I probed indelicately.

"Jeffrey Randall. He's new in town. You wouldn't know him. A widower." Kathryn said curtly.

I looked at her. She was being downright evasive. Jennifer was right. Something was going on.

"You'll meet him eventually," she softened. "You know how it is with us seniors. We don't like to be around you youngsters. Makes us feel old."

We both smiled at this. We would love to be as spry and sharp as she was when we reached our seventies.

Losing Phil had been tough on us all, drawing us closer to Kathryn. A retired stock broker and master gardener, Phil always handed over the first offerings of the season. Like his investments, his garden paid off with bountiful crops for minimum effort. Whatever Phil touched seemed to thrive and multiply whether in a money market account or in the garden. Sometimes he gave us inside tips such as planting shrubs in chicken wire baskets so the main part of the roots would be protected from gophers.

We profited from his tips both in the garden and in our portfolios. But we underestimated Kathryn's role in their partnership until we saw her in action, taking care of her investments with as much, if not more, market expertise than had Phil.

Kathryn started to give the binoculars back to me, but then brought the glasses back to her eyes.

"Thought I saw something else."

"What is it?" Barbara asked and swung the scope into the direction of Kathryn's sighting.

"Nothing. Just one of those apparitions we elders see out of the corner of our eye sometimes. Something that didn't seem to belong there. Something green."

"Might be that parrot," I said.

A happy lory had escaped captivity and adopted our neighborhood, feasting greedily in the fruit trees for the past few summers and sometimes squawking through the air over our heads in exuberant greeting.

"I don't know." Kathryn wagged her head in embarrassment. "My eyesight seems to be compensating for a loss of hearing. Would you believe I saw Phil yesterday? Coming around the garden shed just like he always did on his way in from the garden. Guess he's just a permanent fixture on my eyes."

I nodded in understanding. "You saw him do just that at least a thousand times."

Chapter 4

Barbara and I finally met Jeffrey Randall at a fundraiser for the senior center. It was one of those awful white elephant sales; but being pillars of the community, we felt obligated to support it. We were examining a lamp that sported plastic fibers like giant insect antennae that turned into some kind of laser light show when turned on.

"I think people use them in their den or recreation room," he said.

"Whatever for?" Barbara sniffed.

Randall shrugged, sharing her disdain.

"I have been looking forward to meeting you both. Kathryn has told me all about you."

The favorable first impression was immediately negated by his actually having the audacity to grasp our arms in unwarranted familiarity. Barbara almost hit him. I could see her contain the impulse.

"Yes, we've also been hearing about you." I said, deciding to be civil.

"I'll go get some cider." Barbara dismissed herself, ignoring my glare.

"I hear you're from San Diego."

"Yes. Retired from the service."

Tall, graying and tense, he was somewhere over sixty and fit. Mannered and precise, Randall stopped just short of clicking his heels. He wore an expensive suede jacket and well-tailored gabardine slacks. In a previous era before consciousness was raised about not smoking, he would have smoked a pipe. He didn't seem to fit into Dos Pueblos. Nevertheless, the town was certainly growing fast enough to accommodate lots of affluent retirees from the cities.

"Have you relocated to our town, Mr. Randall?"

"Jeffrey. Please. Yes, I've rented a place out on Zacky Creek. Looking for a little property."

"Not a lot to do here but watch the grass grow."

"I might like to set up something for the homeless here."

"They tend to just keep moving through this area and head for the larger cities."

"That's true of the transients," Jeffrey said. "I'm an administrator for nonprofit organizations, like the senior center here. In San Diego, I ran the local city-wide charitable foundation—CARE and I can tell you the homeless aren't just transients anymore. People with families, even jobs, are getting priced out of the housing market. Even just to rent."

I nodded, wondering how I could agree with him politically, yet feel uneasy with his motivation. Perhaps, I just didn't like his attention to Kathryn so soon after Phil's death. Or his business arrangement for her property.

"We're very fond of Kathryn," I said, not being one to skirt the real agenda.

"Indeed. As I am also. Haven't seen a woman of her spunk since my own wife died over ten years ago."

"Don't worry, CC. Why should I get married when I can have more fun single," Kathryn said as she joined us. "How about some lemonade or cider?"

Although Kathryn seemed perfectly competent to handle her own affairs, I was annoyed that I'd passed up a chance to find out more about Randall's business with Kathryn's property. We'd just finished our drinks when the sound of a rifle shot crackled through the early evening air.

"Was that a gunshot?" Randall asked.

"It's the sniper again," I groaned.

"A sniper?"

"Not really a sniper. Just some fool shoots off his gun from time to time. Driving us all batty."

"Against the law to discharge firearms in the country?"

"Not in the country. But the town is incorporated now and the city limits extend out to our valley."

"Is that where the shots are coming from?"

"Seems to be, but it's hard to tell where it's coming from. Echoes off the hill and down into the valley."

I was repeating what Blakely, the deputy sheriff, had told me when we'd complained about the shots.

"Sounds like a 30-30, a hunting gun." Randall took our paper cups to dispose of them.

"Are you a hunter?" I asked. His domestic gesture of taking our cups had caught me off guard.

He hesitated before answering. "In the past. My father used to take me to the Yolla Bolly mountains. He died in a hunting accident."

I nodded. Somehow, the way he said it, I knew it had been a traumatic incident for him. No doubt he had been present. Just a boy. Perhaps he blamed himself for the accident. But here was the therapist working overtime.

"It must have been difficult for you."

He said nothing. His face revealed no emotion.

Chapter 5

After twenty years, I welcomed disengaging from my clients' lives. I had come to feel like a voyeur, healing vicariously through my clients' recoveries. It had come time for me to get on with the business of my own life.

Birdwatching, wildlife, the weather, all other forms of living things were now accorded a larger place in the scheme of things. It was amazing to me that my world had narrowed so, to what was perceived between the four walls of an office cubicle.

Barbara thought it a splendid idea and after another two years of going off to the classroom, came to see I had the better idea. She also took an early retirement, going on the substitute teacher roster for five or six days a month.

With careful investments and prudent spending habits, we lived modestly. Our expenses were not great. Not working meant not needing new clothes, not buying lunches at restaurants, not filling two cars' tanks with gas every week.

We observed, with interest, this metamorphosis

into a less consumptive lifestyle. Birdwatching and nature walks were inexpensive pursuits, but paid off handsomely in daily dividends of curious and delightful surprises.

"After lunch, let's hike up and have a look at that deer carcass," I proposed.

"You think it will have deteriorated enough?"

"We can take a look." I knew she didn't want to see a bloody, smelly mess. Neither did I. But after two months the vultures, the sun and two rainfalls ought to have eliminated most of the flesh and guts.

New grass was showing green beneath the golden thatch of summer growth, looking like antiqued velvet. The sky had cleared to an incredible blue with cotton candy wisps. I labored up the hill, breathing hard. Barbara was already ahead of me. I get very short winded on an incline. The penalty for having once been a smoker.

The deer hide was like an old dusty rug heaped upon a pile of bones. There was very little odor.

"What's this?" I stooped over the old carcass to retrieve a bullet, flattened and rusty.

Barbara peered nervously around. "That fool sniper must have shot it."

"So he's not using blanks." I put the slug in my pocket.

"Blakely will want to know about this."

"It's a 30-06," he reported that afternoon. "A very common hunting rifle. Must be fifty of them in this valley."

I shuddered at the thought of so many loose cannons in our own backyard.

Chapter 6

"Did you remember that I am going to a conference in La Jolla?" Barbara indicated the calendar page with a Gary Larson cow cartoon on it.

"Am I invited? I like La Jolla with all those lovely shops and it might be cooler on the beach. Also, I could go into San Diego and see what I can find out about Jeffrey Randall. Everytime I see him with Kathryn, I get uneasy. I need to put my mind to rest. And Jennifer's, too."

"Good idea. I'd love to have your company."

Sometimes, like Edna St. Vincent Millay, we went to our conferences alone, welcoming a spot of solitude in our long and lovely association.

We stayed at a fancy hotel by the sea, The Valencia. The water looked like a gigantic vat of purple and turquoise dye. Being close to the ocean was one thing I missed at our inland country kingdom. Although we lived only eighteen miles from the shore, it might as well have been eighty.

I headed out early in the morning. Just past the San Diego Zoo in Balboa Park, I spotted a flash of orangey red in a gingko tree. Despite the cars dashing and darting from lane to lane, I managed to pull over to the side of the road. I would never again complain about traffic on the central coast.

I grabbed binoculars from the glove compartment. Indeed, it was a western tanager, a bird I've seen only once before. Sometimes confused with the oriole, there was no mistaking its red-orange hood, yellow body and black wings. Not with Peterson's field guide sporting its portrait on the cover for so many years.

This had definitely made my day. If my inquiries on Randall didn't amount to anything, seeing a tanager made the struggle through Southern California's traffic worthwhile. Although I was a creature of comfort, I could be a spartan stoic when in pursuit of a worthy quarry.

The CARE office was perched up over Kansas Street, a quiet residential neighborhood. A wheelchair ramp sloped gently up to its ranch-like veranda. The grassy berm was well-maintained with borders of yellow and gold zinnias and rusty red dahlias in an autumnal design.

CARE's reception area looked like a doctor's waiting room. I scanned the magazines.

"I like your outfit. Liz Claiborne?" I asked the mature woman in pleated slacks and a sweater with padded shoulders who greeted me pleasantly, asking me to take a seat while she got someone to help me. The plaque on her desk read Mildred Modriani.

"Yes, and on sale. Isn't she wonderful?"

We beamed in understanding of the years gone by of suffering through girdles, garters, panty hose and high heels. None of these were as fashionable anymore as relaxed natural fabrics.

And in my semi-retired state, I was even beginning to prefer wearing baggy corduroy trousers, an oversized shirt and long cotton cardigan.

"Have you worked here long?" Maybe she knew Randall.

"Ten years." She smiled. "I retired once but couldn't bear the idleness. I just do this part time now. Have grandchildren to look after. My daughter is a lawyer now," she added.

I nodded.

"You might have know someone then. Jeffrey Randall?"

"Well, of course. He was our director for some five years. Did a fine job, too. Everyone thought very highly of him."

I watched Mildred roll a piece of stationary into her electronic typewriter. I remained quiet, hoping there might be more.

"Well, I didn't think he was Mr. Perfect like everyone else. I was his secretary, so I saw the real person with all his warts." She took her gold-rimmed glasses off to look at me. "Quite the ladies' man. But not my type if you know what I mean."

I guessed Jeffrey may have been a bit too efficient for her, that she would prefer someone less precise and more jolly.

"Why do you think he left?" I dared to ask.

Mildred was silent, appearing to weigh her response. I waited, having learned early in my practice that the less I said, the more the other person would talk.

"I think Jeffrey is the kind of man that needs new

challenges. Things were going too well around here. Sometimes I think he was just looking for something to go wrong so he could fix it. Jeffrey seemed to be bored."

I nodded. "Yes, I've known people like that. Don't think they're alive unless they have a problem to attend to."

"Exactly."

Further confidences seemed forthcoming, however a man in a navy three-piece suit entered the room, introducing himself as the assistant director and apologizing for my wait. But he proved to be a disappointing resource, citing confidentiality or lack of information for every one of my questions.

Chapter 7

"He was unctuous," I reported later to Barbara in our spacious La Jolla hotel room. "He made Jeffrey look good by comparison."

"Who is the director now?" Barbara asked.

"That's the puzzling thing. There's been no director since Jeffrey left. The chairman of the board is serving as interim director and the unctuous assistant handles the daily operations."

"After six months?" she asked as she nestled into a thick terry cloth robe, compliments of the house. Fifty dollars on your bill if you wanted to take it home.

"Apparently they've offered the job to several candidates, but they all wind up declining for one reason or another."

"What about the assistant?"

I had to grin at that. "Not a leader of men, or women. It almost looks like Jeffrey was so good they can't fill his shoes and when they try, the candidates themselves balk. Apparently Jeffrey Randall was a very accomplished administrator."

"No women candidates?" Barbara helped herself to the tea service.

"No women. Too bad. The receptionist was probably the most qualified."

"What now?"

I could hear what she was thinking. Four more days to go here and I'd hit a dead end so far as she could see.

"Oh, I'll find out why those candidates backed out. Look them up and ask."

"How can you even find out who they are much less where they are?" she asked with an air of finality. She seemed to see the matter as closed.

"Since CARE is a non-profit organization, the meetings are public and the minutes are of record."

"But where?" Barbara sprinkled sugar in her tea.

"CARE should make the minutes available to anyone who asks." I said, thinking out loud. "But they would probably decline to furnish them to someone who didn't have a legitimate reason to know."

Inviting Mildred to lunch the next day was the easy part. We met in a small garden cafe near the north end of the park. I watched her get out of a black Cadillac. It was amazing how executive secretaries could look more the role than their bosses.

The hard part was coming up with a story to justify my request. I was forced to resort to the truth.

"So, as much as I hate to put you on the spot, I really need to know that Mr. Randall's intentions are honorable."

Our lunch finished, we lingered over the coffee, a rich Kenya bean. Mildred was silent. I respected her need to think about such a request.

"I could let you have the names and phone numbers of two of the top candidates," Mildred said. "I agree you have a legitimate need to know. But you don't really need to have the minutes."

I was happy. This was good enough.

Chapter 8

"Just like that she gives you their names and phone numbers?" Barbara was quite surprised.

"Well, I think she came to trust that I wouldn't use the names or numbers for any purpose other than to find out why these guys balked at taking the directorship when it was offered to them."

"Now what?"

"I have messages into their answering machines. We wait."

The first call came about halfway through a National Geographic special on plate tectonics in East Africa. With a pleasant and curious voice he identified himself as Matthew Sorens and asked how he might help me. I had left my name and hotel number with the message that I needed to talk with him about his experience at CARE.

Initially he hesitated. "That's highly confidential information. I would need to know more about you and why you wanted to know."

I proposed meeting for coffee the next morning after assuring him that my reasons for wanting to know were not nefarious.

Barbara shook her head and turned her attention back to East Africa geography. "I can't believe how people just fall under your spell, CC."

"Just your basic forthrightness. Gets them every time."

We were in the hotel's coffee shop, dipping into a buffet of fruit and pastries. It was nine-thirty in the morning and Matthew Sorens had appeared on time. He was a slightly built forty-year old, attired in tan corduroy jacket and brown slacks with a checked shirt and sports tie.

"You mean Randall was *too* good?"

"Yes. It's embarrassing to admit. But taking that job would have ruined my career. I would never have measured up to Randall's performance."

"Isn't it peculiar, though, that at least two of you backed out at the last minute."

"I can't speak for anyone else, but it was only when they offered the job that I was allowed to see the books. Randall's financial performance was outstanding. The best I've ever seen for a nonprofit corporation." He buttered a piece of bran muffin.

"What exactly did you see?" I signaled the waiter for more coffee.

"I can't say anymore than that, Ms. Scott, without violating an executive trust. You understand, I hope."

"Cynthia. Just call me CC. And of course, I understand. I'm very grateful you would consent to meet with me and tell me as much as you have."

We fell silent as the waiter refilled our cups.

"But I need to be frank with you, Mr. Sorens."

"Matt," he prompted.

"I think there was something shady going on. Maybe not illegal, but not quite ethical either."

"Mmmm. There is a gray area between the two in many dealings," Matt admitted. "If that is so, it would certainly vindicate me," he mused aloud.

"Then you had just such a thought cross your own mind?" I asked.

"Yes," he hesitated. "But CARE is a highly regarded agency. It funds many of the county's community services—the women's shelter, developmentally disabled, the teen center. You don't cast aspersions on something that does so much for so many. That would blackball me in this town. Make me look like a bad guy. Besides I have no proof."

"Proof of what?"

He smiled indulgently at my persistence. "Of anything illegal."

"Why do you think Randall left if things were going so well?"

Matt shrugged. "Five years is about a normal life span for nonprofit administrators. We like to move on to new agencies. It's the only way to get significant salary jumps."

I nodded. Of course. A director couldn't ask a nonprofit board for a sizeable increase without looking self-serving.

"If he was engaged in questionable tactics, he might have feared exposure," I ventured.

"From whom? No one would want to touch it. Not even a muckraking newspaper reporter." Matt rose to leave. “I’m sorry, but I have another appointment, an interview, and must go. I’ve been unemployed longer than I care to say.”

Chapter 9

After getting back from La Jolla, we heard from the second candidate, Guy Rathborne, who lived in Carmel. I took the call in the study, looking out the window at our orchard, the trees bowing with fruit. We talked only briefly, but the connection was an occasion for events to take a pleasant turn, at least for now.

“I’m sorry, Ms. Scott. There isn’t anything else to tell you. I decided not to take the job because my partner and I have established a home here in Carmel Valley and I would have had to commute on weekends,” he said with clipped words.

But he had to know that going into the interview. I thought it peculiar that he changed his mind after being offered the position. And I didn’t miss his reference to a partner. That usually meant an unmarried mate. I decided to take a chance.

"Of course. That's hard on a relationship. My partner and I have never lived apart in twenty years. She would never permit it."

"Ah. We are family." His attitude did a complete turnabout.

"I have reason to believe Jeffrey Randall may have been engaged in some questionable practices during his tenure at CARE. I had hoped that you might have seen or heard something during your interviews there."

"I don't think we should discuss this on the phone."

"We would be happy to come to Carmel if you would see us."

Barbara had entered the study and nodded her assent.

We agreed to meet for dinner at The Pines in Carmel the following Saturday evening. Guy said he would make reservations, his demeanor now warm and charming.

"Now you've finagled us a social invitation out of all this," Barbara said amused. "The length to which you will go to evade boredom."

"You like Carmel almost as much as I like La Jolla. Besides, we'll probably have to pay for dinner if he's still in between jobs." I grinned at her to let her know I didn't care one way or another.

One of those quiet moments of happiness passed between us. When we first got together so many years ago, I used to wonder what this peculiar feeling was stealing over me. It took me awhile to realize it was plain old unadorned love. I liked it a lot. It was not taken for granted that we had the luxury of each other's companionship and were still best friends.

In her lycra workout suit, Barbara looked like a professional athlete with great biceps and ample thighs, her face cheerfully pink-cheeked from her recent exertion of a bicycle ride. Straight black hair, Indian hair, she called it, was beginning to soften with frosted touches of gray. Laugh lines twinkled at the corners of her brown eyes and generous mouth.

Impulsively, I went to her to kiss her fulsomely on the mouth. She wrapped me in her arms, as always, and kissed me back.

Chapter 10

"I think Randall was skimming because he lived so well on such a modest salary." Guy waved a fork full of salad. A squat chunky man, he looked like a miniature weight lifter. He bristled with more than his share of testosterone.

"How does that explain his success on the profit ledger at CARE?" Barbara asked.

We all helped ourselves to the fragrant warm sourdough from the basket on the table.

"If he was skimming, then you would think the organization would not be so healthy." I followed up Barb's question.

Guy looked at his partner. Armando was a black

charismatic presence. He'd modestly admitted to being *the* Armando Corral, a San Francisco opera baritone, when Barbara recognized him. Armando nodded encouragement, flashing his dazzling smile.

"I'm not sure, but it looked to me like there were a lot of rich widows on the board of directors. Right off I noticed the board wasn't truly representative of the community. It wasn't a cross section of the population."

I nodded. This had promise.

"Maybe some gay men would find nothing wrong with cultivating the largesse of elderly, affluent women, but not me," Guy said, "I belong more in the locker room."

"I didn't want you to commute, either," Armando spoke up. "Especially for a job that didn't look that good. I'd rather keep you in the style to which we've become accustomed."

Guy grinned at his partner. "I can always go back to fishing."

"Not while I'm in port."

It seemed to be a private joke.

"How did you two get together?" I asked. Like many couples we viewed the exchanging of romantic history as a way of acknowledging each other's marriages.

"A bar in San Francisco, before AIDS," Guy spoke up. "I really was deep sea fishing then. I'd just come into port and here was this magnificent Othello."

"I'd come from a performance, and in walks this banty-legged little macho butch."

"It was lust at first sight," Guy said. "She was a gorgeous sight after weeks of looking at ugly seamen."

Barbara and I smiled and nodded.

"What about you two?" Armando asked.

"We met at school," Barbara began.

"Stanford?" Guy interrupted.

"Yes. How did you know?" I was surprised.

"Barbara is wearing an old Indian pin." Guy pointed to the gold gleam on her jacket.

She grinned. "I didn't know but what we'd need a little extra leverage into the old boys' network."

"I rather liked the Indian symbol," Armando asserted, "but I can certainly appreciate the civil rights consciousness that led to changing it to the Cardinals."

"How about Stanford Dykes?" I joked.

"It has a certain cachet," Guy admitted, "but Stanford Fairies would be even better when you consider what they do on the football field."

Hilarious laughter accompanied the serving of our entree. I'm sure the waiter wondered how in the world we could be having such a good time without anything alcoholic to drink.

Our lightheartedness covered up the difficulties of being gay in America, especially back in the late fifties when we came out. Then, being a queer was worse than being a commie pinko. The fear of being found out, of being labeled deviants, was to lose one's place in the community with a seriousness akin to an Eskimo being left on an ice floe. And, on the practical side Barbara risked losing her scholarship.

"What you saw in San Diego jibes with what we are seeing in Dos Pueblos." I brought us back to the subject at hand after dessert, a decadent chocolate torte. We had consumed it in reverential silence.

"Randall is offering to pay our neighbor's mortgage and maintenance in return for her bequest of the property."

"Living trusts!" Guy exclaimed. "So that's why all the huge one time bequests."

"What do you mean, Guy?" I was paying attention. We were on to something here.

"Usually you don't want only one time bequests. You want many small continuing donations. Otherwise, your very existence is at risk to those few benefactors' whims. They may decide to donate to United Way the following year."

"But if you have many rich widows whose estates are fattening the purse on a regular basis?" Barbara asked.

"Then you don't need so many fundraisers," Guy said. "Although it looked like Randall did his share of events. Big ones, too."

"But what can you do at this stage?" Armando asked rhetorically. "None of this is illegal."

"We can wait and watch. He'll slip up somewhere." I was determined. And knowing what Guy had seen in the financial ledgers now made the vigilance imperative.

Driving home from Carmel, Barbara reminisced about our early courtship. "Do you remember when we were necking in the dorm shower and Priscilla Whitehorn walked in?"

"That's when we knew we had to get an apartment, immediately." I smiled to remember the dizzy happiness of those early days.

Barbara was a splendid recompense for a life that up to that point had been difficult. My father's perpetual depressions had afflicted the entire family. Calvin, my brother, and I had had to tiptoe through adolescence, dreading doing anything to set him off on another morose spell.

In exact counterpoint, Barbara was a joyful person with none of the downs that sometimes accompany that personality. Steady and even tempered, her emotional states were easy and reliable. I never had to worry about what she was feeling. What she was thinking was another matter.

I reached over to place my hand on her leg. A sensation of sensuous warmth rewarded me, tingling my nerve endings even after all this time. Her new wool slacks were especially fetching on her, the fit showing off her long legs and cute bottom.

Today Kenneth Scott would be clinically diagnosed as depressed. He'd be put on medication and would be able to live a normal life. Or a good therapist would help him dig down inside and find out why he was depressed and aid him to heal himself.

But my father's generation found it unthinkable to see a therapist. It meant you were crazy. Rather than admit a problem, he stayed miserable and became worse. When he died three years ago, I was sorry to say that the most I felt was relief. I would not have to worry about him anymore.

Outwardly, he had been a successful corporate executive at a small electronics firm, but inwardly a misfit, a misplaced person. A Stanford man, he had conformed to the gray flannel suit when, I suspected, it was an artist's beret he had wanted.

My father's good manners could not mask the fundamental morbidity that he had taken a wrong turn in life. Dutifully he had assisted Calvin and me through Stanford. He had taken a polite interest in our studies, but no real joy or pride in us. We had felt barely tolerated.

My mother, Patricia Chenery originally from a privileged upstate New York family, had provided the extras of life both materially and maternally. She had lavished affection and toys and books on us. Like Barbara, mother was of a buoyant disposition, which was no doubt why father had been drawn to her in the first place.

Barbara responded to my hand on her leg, tracing my fingers with her own elegant touch as we drove through the night with the meditation music of Kitaro on the cassette tape.

If the theory was true that we grow up to be like one of our parents and marry the other, then I had, indeed, married my mother. Barbara never brooded about injustice or unfairness, as I did from time to time. I was grateful, however, that my moodiness was a much milder version of father's depression. This was probably no accident. My choice of psychotherapy as a field was no doubt an attempt to ameliorate my own propensity to despair.

Also, I had discovered two important coping mechanisms. One was not to drink alcohol. The other was to get some physical exercise at least three or four times a week. I had learned over the years, too, that the survival strategies I came to teach clients were precisely the things I needed to practice myself. We teach what we need to learn or something like that.

"You better stop that or we won't make it home." My tingles were beginning to border on something more demanding. Filling the car with slow sensuous sounds, a Bach etude had replaced the Kitaro.

Thinking about my mother had reminded me to call her the following morning to see how she was faring after a minor surgery—a small benign cyst on her arm. She continued to live in our family homestead in Ventura, doing her good works of service for the Salvation Army. Mom had readily accepted my taking on a woman as a life partner. If she'd had any private misgivings, she had the grace to never let on to either of us. I loved her for that.

We drove on through the night, snug and temporarily safe in a cocoon of our own making, wrapped in the music of Bach.

Chapter 11

I happened to be at the office supply store when Kathryn and another woman came in.

"CC, I want you to meet Vera McAndrews. She's the new assistant director at Shelterworks," Kathryn said, turning to her friend.

I put down the stationery I was examining and stepped forward to greet this rather imposing looking woman with honey blonde hair swept back into a tidy roll at the back of her head. Her hand was firm and warm.

"Is that the new agency for the homeless?" Randall hadn't wasted any time.

"Yes. We're ordering supplies for the board of directors. Kathryn has agreed to serve."

Kathryn glowed happily, holding a clipboard with what looked to be an office shopping list.

"I was going to tell you over the weekend but I was so busy, what with the senior center and now the board."

"You mean you already have a facility?"

"Yes, it's being refurbished right now. Paint. Furniture. The works," Vera said as she adjusted the Cassini scarf accenting her navy blue suit.

"My goodness. However did it happen so fast? This county takes months to do these things, not weeks." I said duly impressed, having had a few dealings with our local health services.

"Jeffrey. Mr. Randall has kicked things off with his own money. He calls it good faith money. County and state funds will follow."

"And what exactly will be your area of responsibility?" I asked Vera.

"I'll be running the shelter itself and interviewing candidates for the self-help building program."

"A building program? That's good news."

"Yes. It's going to be a wonderful program. I had almost given up finding anything like this. I was getting desperate, running out of money."

"She was the best out of fifty candidates," Kathryn contributed.

"Which is hard to believe since jobs are so hard to come by around here. I recently went back to school to get a degree in public health administration. My experience has actually been in the secretarial arena."

"Not to be underestimated." I noted.

"I've always wanted to help other people. I've been down myself."

I must have given her a subtle signal of understanding.

"Each time I see someone else get back on their feet, I relive my own recovery."

There was the air of the religious convert about her, but I knew it was sincere.

"I know what you mean."

"Of course you do. Kathryn tells me you are a therapist."

"A semi-retired one."

"What is your specialty?"

"Post traumatic stress disorder. Dysfunctional families."

"Oh, wonderful. Perhaps we can engage you as a consultant in the near future."

"Sure, I'd love to be of assistance." I imagined it would buy a few groceries. "I've had some experience with Viet Nam Vets and alcoholics, too," I said as I thought about the chance to get an inside look at Randall.

"Good. Just what we need. May I call you?"

"Of course." I had to admit that Vera was a mover and a shaker, too. She and Randall must make a good team.

We were blocking the aisle between the stacks of notepads and stationery and another customer came down the aisle.

"Is that you Vera? You look gorgeous!" said Petey, the waitress from the coffee shop.

"Oh, Petey." Vera put out her arms and they hugged carefully.

"This is Kathryn..."

"Sure, I know both Kathryn and CC. How are you?" She waved her hand in a friendly gesture. Petey knew everyone in town.

"Well, how's it doing? Are you going to be able to handle him?"

Vera frowned. "Kathryn is on our board and CC may be serving as a consultant."

"We know Jeffrey's difficult, Vera. You don't have to pussyfoot on our account," Kathryn piped up.

She relaxed. "He is a strange duck, isn't he?"

"A bit of a chauvinist?" That was what I'd suspected all along, beneath his suave exterior.

"Maybe something ... deeper." Vera searched for the right word. My therapist antennae went on full alert.

"What do you mean?" We had all unconsciously lowered our voices to a whisper.

"Whacko?" Petey asked.

"Not that extreme. Just a bit off center."

"Well, aren't we all?" This from Kathryn jerked at my awareness.

Suddenly I saw us, four gossipy women, hissing in a corner about some pathetic man. Of course, if we were men, it would be called a conference.

"I suppose we are." Vera looked at me in an appeal for understanding.

"Some of us are more off center than others." I didn't want us to be too easy on him.

"But you've come a long ways, my friend." Petey turned to Vera again.

"It's a hard job, waitressing."

"To make a living at it, it is," Petey admitted. "But I just play at it. I enjoy the socializing of it."

"Besides, Normand makes plenty of money," Vera said. A part of her apparently still subscribed to the notion that a woman's worth was tied to whether her man could support her. The idea seemed inconsistent with her own career action.

"Right. Which reminds me. He told me to tell you not to get high and mighty on us now that you're a big shot executive."

"Oh, he did, did he? Well, he's in big trouble. We're going to need a good electrical contractor for the building program. I'm counting on him."

"You better come to dinner Sunday and talk him into it." Petey challenged her.

"Okay. I'll be there. With my instruments of torture and persuasion."

"A six pack will do it. He's easy."

Kathryn smiled at me, letting me know she was aware of how it affects a non-drinking person to be constantly besieged with the culture's drinking practices. I shrugged to let her know it was okay.

"This center is getting a lot of people involved," I observed after Petey left.

"Yes. That's how it should be. The community should own it and run it." Vera turned back to the shelves of supplies.

"Is that the latest helping agency theory?" I like it.

"Yes. The more broad based the involvement, the more empowered the community becomes to solve its own social problems."

"Could that extend to drug and alcohol problems, too?" This had great merit.

"Yes, indeed. We're not solving addiction problems by throwing government money at it, or waging war. We have to go to the supply source and consumption attitudes." Vera put some notepads and file folders in her basket.

"Like those neighborhood watch programs in Oakland and New York?"

"Whatever it takes for each community. Dos Pueblos doesn't have the big city problems but there are things that community activism could affect."

"Like what?" Kathryn joined in.

"Like selling alcohol at service stations. It sends a message that it's okay to drink and drive, especially to young people."

I had to agree. Vera McAndrews was most impressive. No wonder she had gotten the job.

"Same with the homeless. We need to take care of our own with what is actually needed, what is appropriate, not what some bureaucrats in Washington have decided is the national average."

"What do you have in mind for our alcoholics and mentally ill?" I asked.

"Information and referral, so far. But that's where your consultation could help. You could advise us as to what programs are available and what we need to provide ourselves."

"I'll do some thinking on it." This looked like it would be more of a challenge than I thought. It meant evaluating existing services and proposing new ones.

Chapter 12

I was tending Donal Sanders' patients while he went on a European vacation. Lulled into therapy as usual, I was surprised by an emergency call late in the afternoon.

"I feel like I'm going to explode," he said into the phone.

I made sure he was not in danger of doing harm to himself or others, then recommended a bowl of soup and a hot bath. Jasper Willard agreed to perform these acts of caring for himself and to appear at ten o'clock in the morning for a session.

"I feel better already just talking to you and knowing you can see me," he'd said in a raspy voice.

It was the same for me when I had a toothache and made an appointment with my pretty dentist.

The next morning, I saw him come in for his appointment. He took off a grain and feed cap to show a receding forehead shiny with perspiration. He was a stringy man, nervous and tense, wearing a Pendleton shirt and Levis, the customary rancher's dress clothes.

He seemed afraid to fill out the registration form, so I scooped up the form and introduced myself, giving him a good firm handshake. He seemed reassured.

Once inside the office, he looked around at the small desk and three comfortable chairs with lamps and bookshelves that made a cozy sitting room.

"I thought there would be a couch."

I smiled and nodded. "Guess they did in the old days."

"You're not what I expected," he grinned back at me.

"Someone younger, perhaps?"

"Yes. Everyone is getting too young."

I nodded, knowing what he meant. Doctors, police, bank presidents, everyone seemed so young as we got older. Like juvenile birds that were bigger than the parents tending them. It was unnerving when you were accustomed to seeing persons in positions of authority as older and wiser than oneself. It was especially unsettling to see them younger and no more competent than oneself. Or worse yet, perhaps less. For a rancher, it must be doubly hard to have confidence in young twerps when the very nature of farming is to do things for yourself.

"Did you sleep better last night?" I got on with the session.

"Yes. That's exactly what my wife would have done. Fix me a bowl of soup."

"Is she gone?"

"Died six months ago." There was no emotion in his voice. "Cancer. She went fast, but we had forty wonderful years together and plenty of time to say goodbye."

I sensed he was saying he shouldn't grieve her dying.

"I manage all right, even though things aren't the same."

"Do you have other family?"

"Yes, and they have been wonderful. The daughters took turns staying with me. The boys came out to the ranch on weekends. Helped me get the alfalfa in. The family rallied around. We're closer than ever."

But now it's all worn off and reality is setting in, I thought.

"Do you have plans for the holidays?" I asked as a sharp stab of feeling hit me that someday Barb and I would be faced with the same problem. One of us would die first and the other one would have to go on alone.

"There's something else," he hesitated.

"Yes." I was quiet and waited.

"I'm the one who has been firing a rifle out in Lucca Valley. I need to stop it. It's just blanks," he added lamely.

"A twenty-one gun salute." I was delighted.

"You don't think I'm crazy?"

"No. I think you're focusing anger at losing your wife into shooting the rifle. Could even be a kind of farewell to her. A twenty-one gun salute."

"Like Kennedy or a war hero?" He grinned, seeing his own drama.

"Exactly." I was pleased. Now he could grasp the notion that his choked back grief would have to find a way of expressing itself. And the prospect of having to end the random shooting was an extra dividend.

"Let yourself grieve for your wife. What is her name?"

"Abigail. Abby, we called her." His eyes filled with tears.

"Let the tears come, instead of the rifle," I said softly, knowing he was right on the edge.

Jasper began to cry mightily and noisily, sobbing hard for a long time. A lifetime of accumulated losses pouring out in one huge crying jag.

I moved closer to him letting him know I was near but not interfering with his therapeutic need to cry.

When he began to wind down, I handed him some tissues and put my arm around him, wincing at the piercing through to my own inner core of pain.

"I must have needed that." Jasper could say with a wry grin. He was returning to normal with his ego defenses back in place.

I was respectful and nodded, allowing myself some recovery time, too.

"Probably a whole lifetime accumulated in that one good cry," I said.

"I feel better," he admitted. "Maybe I ought to come back for another session though?"

"Only if you feel the need to talk to someone," I said. "Or if you don't stop shooting off the rifle." I carefully refrained from saying *can't stop shooting off the rifle*.

He nodded. "I can stop now. It was just blanks but I know it had folks worried."

"Are you sure about the blanks?" I was now afraid his confession had created more questions than it had provided answers.

"Oh, yes. I've always used blanks because of the kids being around but I need a gun to scare off dogs."

"Do you have sheep?"

"Yes. Blackface."

One of the hazards of living in the country was that some people felt they had a right to let their dogs loose at night. But the dogs ganged together in packs, roaming the neighboring ranches for easy prey like sheep and goats, to slaughter senselessly.

As Jasper left the office he turned back to me. "You won't tell anyone about me."

"Of course not. Everything is held in highest confidentiality," I assured him. "Nothing you have said can be disclosed to anyone else."

Here was a dilemma, indeed. If the rifle shots stopped, then there would be no need to be concerned. If Jasper didn't stop, I would then have to grapple with the ethics of whether his actions are a danger to himself or others. Probably not. Yet that had been a real bullet in the blacktail on the hill.

Grief-crazed or drinking, he could forget to put blanks in, or just plain make a mistake. A stray bullet could kill as sure as if it had been aimed. Just recently someone had been target shooting on his own property. A bullet had gone over a hill, descended, bounced off a wheelbarrow and struck a little girl at play in her yard. The two ranches had not even been in sight of one another.

"Mr. Willard." I called him back in the hallway. "What kind of rifle do you have?"

"Winchester 30-30."

I nodded, leaving him free to go. Blakely had said my deer slug was a 30-06.

I contented myself for now with writing up the case for Dr. Sanders, explaining the problem and our need to consult if there were any shots in the future.

It would be easy for Blakely to check on Jasper's gun if it happened again. Somehow I believed Jasper was telling the truth. Someone else shot the deer on our hill.

Chapter 13

In the country if you were any kind of gardener and you heard of a free supply of compost or manure, you would gladly borrow a truck and go get it. That was my mission this morning. Kicking an old V 8 pickup into life and heading across the valley to the west side to a mushroom farm. There was something about the power in a truck. I could feel it in the seat of my jeans. I could see why men like to drive them. And now, of course, lots of women, too.

Shady Valley Mushrooms. The sign said where to turn onto a gravel road. I'd taken these mushrooms home from the supermarket many times. They were always the freshest. Plump and white and firm in heaps so I could pick out the best ones.

On this side of the valley, the air was cooler, the morning sun filtered by a forest of giant oaks and

Digger pines. A good location for a mushroom farm. Spanish moss draped languidly from the oaks and acorn woodpeckers swooped by in flashes of red and white and black.

A car, a Mercedes, was parked alongside the road on a shoulder. It looked familiar. I slowed down, in case someone was having car trouble and needed help. The lid to the luggage deck was raised, but no one was in sight. Maybe they had engine trouble and had walked up to the farm to call for assistance.

It was slow coming, but it dawned on me I'd seen that car before, next door. It was Randall's. I hit the brakes and pulled over. What in the world was he doing out here? Perhaps looking at land. He'd said he was looking for property.

I was in no hurry. I could wait for him. But I couldn't stand it. What was that man doing here? I got out of the truck and poked around on either side of the road, walking in far enough to get past the trees that screened the fields from view.

There he was. In a meadow by an old farmhouse, one of the early settlers' places. He had a lot of camera equipment draped about him. Then I remembered he was a photographer. The wildflower slides. But there were no wildflowers this time of the year. What was he shooting?

I stayed behind the trees edging the meadow. He was about a football field's distance away. If I stayed still, he wouldn't see me. And if he headed back this way, I could just leave ahead of him. I lamented not having my binoculars.

Randall seemed to be studying the old farmhouse looking for the best camera angle. I could tell him already the light was all wrong to bring out the texture of the old house. What he needed was softer light, early evening light. It was too brilliant this morning. The detail would contrast out. If he was any kind of photographer, he would know that. But what did I know? Maybe he was after a high intensity image.

I saw him drop the camera from his face. Then he gathered up his equipment and headed in my direction. I couldn't explain why I didn't scoot then and get in the truck and drive away. Some momentary madness.

But I waited in the trees until he'd walked past me, my heart pounding. He looked at the truck with passing curiosity, then slung his camera equipment in the deck with uncommon roughness. I shouldn't have been surprised. People do all sorts of strange things when they think no one is watching. But I would never throw expensive cameras and lenses around like that.

When I returned home with my load of mushroom compost, I did a double take to see Randall's car again, next door at Kathryn's. I parked the truck behind our barn so he wouldn't see it.

Not being inclined to mind my own business, I went right over, grabbing a half dozen eggs to take to her.

"Hello, CC. You remember Jeffrey Randall, don't you?"

Kathryn was dressed to go out in plaid wool slacks, a turtleneck of Phil's and a cardigan sweater. She usually just wore jeans and sweatshirts around the house, just like us, having come to appreciate the comfort.

"Of course. I hear you've already launched your

new agency."

"Yes, it's coming along very nicely."

I could tell he was uncomfortable. Behind him on the dining room table were papers, legal papers.

"Jeffrey is taking me to Dr. Phyllis and then to lunch at the Rialto."

"The doctor's? Nothing serious, I hope."

"Just the usual ticker check up." Kathryn touched her chest on the left side like she was saying the pledge of allegiance. Since Phil had died she had developed an erratic heartbeat that needed frequent monitoring.

"I just wanted to deliver your eggs before you got away." I tried to edge closer to the dining room table as I headed for the kitchen.

"Thanks, CC. I'll take them." Kathryn intercepted me.

I looked anyway. It was apparent what they were. Real estate documents.

"Kathryn and I are just taking care of a little business. Did you know that she is going to serve on our board?" Jeffrey had noticed my attention.

"Yes. So I heard. I met your new assistant a few days ago." I could see Kathryn had already signed. I was too late.

"A charitable investment trust," Jeffrey explained. "Kathryn is doing some estate planning that benefits both the agency and herself."

I had a flash of annoyance for his smug explanation.

"What happens if another director takes over Shelterworks?"

"The contract is ironclad. Kathryn is guaranteed her right to residency for the rest of her life."

"What if she becomes ill and has to go to a convalescent home?"

"Shelterworks takes care of all her needs, whether medical or material."

"How can your agency afford to do this?" I just didn't get it.

"Most people don't have extraordinary expenses." He seemed sincere, intent in making me understand this was a good thing for Kathryn.

"Just like insurance companies. We play the averages. There are many people making such bequests, but only a few having unusual expenses. The gain outweighs the costs."

"I thought of having my lawyer look these papers over before I signed them," Kathryn came back from the kitchen. "But I mistrust lawyers more than I do Jeffrey. He seems to know what he is doing." She handed me the empty egg carton.

"It tickles me no end to avoid tax consequences."

I could imagine so. Kathryn's assets were now quite substantial. The house and acreage were only a small part of her estate. Kathryn and Phil were the kind of people who went to some trouble not to flaunt their affluence to their friends and neighbors. My mother was like that. Just because one could afford to buy something didn't mean it was necessary to do so.

"Besides, Jeffrey hasn't fooled me for one minute. Now that he's got me signed up, he'll be checking out the other ladies at the senior center." She grinned at the moment of discomfort on his face.

"Kathryn. Kathryn. How could you think so ill of me?" Jeffrey recovered himself. "Above all others I hold thee." He made a courtly bow to her.

"That will do. We better get to the doctor's." Kathryn grinned at his antics.

Outside her door a family of quail marched up the driveway. We stopped to watch them.

"They look like wind up toys," Kathryn observed.

"But their faces are fierce with warrior paint." I looked at Randall to see if he got my drift. I think he did.

Chapter 14

"Shelterworks will pay you fifty dollars an hour for your time." Vera was wearing a gray wool dress, another designer scarf and classic pumps. She looked like an administrator.

Vera McAndrews had phoned me to come in and discuss the terms of my consulting for the program.

"What about the time I've already spent evaluating existing resources?" It hadn't been a lot, but neither did I want to sell myself too cheaply.

"How much time are we talking about?" Vera looked down at her papers. I figured she must have an allowance for this expenditure.

"Two hours at the most."

"No problem. If you agree to the terms, we'll include those hours." She made a note on what looked to be my timesheet.

"Agreed." This was to be a new experience my ego could not refuse. Besides it gave me an inside track to keep an eye out for Kathryn. Not that I'd done so well so far. Having to explain to Jennifer I let her aunt sign away the property had been downright humbling.

Randall himself appeared at Vera's office door.

"Something's come up. I have to leave for the day." He nodded at me, all business like.

"Would you like me to cancel the meeting?"

He hesitated. "You can handle it. The agenda is fairly simple. Tell them I've had a personal emergency."

"I'm sorry. Is there anything else I can do to help?" Vera was quite caring toward him. It was like a marriage. An office marriage.

"No. But thank you." His voice was husky, his eyes avoided me.

If Dos Pueblos had been a larger town I would not have seen him ten minutes later at the bank. I'd left Vera to attend to her appointments and gone to the bank to deposit a few dividend checks. I ducked behind a potted plant, feeling like a fool.

"Moving assets around a bit," he told the teller. I saw a large amount of cash which he tucked into a nine by twelve manilla envelope.

I stayed behind the palm for thirty seconds, then followed him out. He roared away in his Mercedes. I couldn't seem to stop myself from just doing what came naturally. I followed him. I was pretty sure he hadn't ever seen our little import car since we keep it in the garage.

He went to the Texaco gas station. His Mercedes was a diesel model. I stayed down the street, parked with my motor running. My heart raced, too. I knew he had to be up to something important to skip a board meeting.

When he pulled out of the station, I followed two car lengths behind. I would have told a client that this was obsessive behavior.

His speed picked up on the highway to sixty, seventy miles an hour, much faster than I like to go, especially in some of California's prettiest scenery of green rolling hills studded with huge oak trees.

Then past San Luis to the coast where Pismo Beach curves along the sand. Eighty miles an hour now. Much too fast for me. I had to drop back. I gave up and took an off ramp. Barbara would wonder what took me so long. I didn't want to worry her. He was obviously headed out of town. San Diego came to mind.

As I headed back to Dos Pueblos, fog swirled over the highway and a ghostly seagull glided by my window.

Chapter 15

It was only two days later that Kathryn begged for us to join her and Randall at dinner. We disliked the prospect of spending an evening with him but it was impossible to say no to Kathryn's invitation. We met at the Rialto Hotel, her favorite restaurant. Barbara and I were both on guard.

"We'll be electing officers at our next meeting," said Kathryn. Her excitement was electric.

"I'm planning on Kathryn being one of those elected officers." Jeffrey looked up from his dinner.

"You mean you know ahead of time who is going to be elected?" Barbara asked.

Jeffrey looked pained. He'd probably been asked this before.

"No, of course not. But like any election, there is lobbying and some candidates are considered more appropriate than others. Then there are nominations and a period of suitable getting acquainted with the nominees. Seeing how they operate under pressure, as it were."

He paused to take a drink of water, perspiration evident on his high forehead.

"Only then is there a balloted election. Quite an involved process."

"It is important for the officers to all share a common vision," Kathryn spoke up.

Barbara and I looked at each other. We could hear a quote from Jeffrey if there ever was one.

He was silent, delving into his entree of lamb chops in raspberry sauce.

"Wouldn't Phil be surprised," Kathryn bubbled. "Me, the chairman of the board."

"He always did admire your head for business," I reminded her.

"When did you retire from psychotherapy?" Jeffrey quickly asked to change the topic.

I couldn't respond right away, having just taken a mouthful of beef tenderloin on artichoke hearts.

"She isn't really retired," Kathryn explained for me. "She does vacation relief for other psychologists."

"Where did you take your training?" he continued smoothly. The object of his attentions was apparent.

"Stanford for graduate school and the Veteran's hospital for my internship. Where did you go to school, Mr. Randall?" I asked in turn.

"Jeffrey, please. I'm actually a self-educated man although I did get a degree at San Diego. What is your specialty?" He returned to me relentlessly.

"Post traumatic stress disorder." I studied him, wondering why he was so interested. "Vietnam veterans when I first started out and then later, children of dysfunctional families."

He nodded. We might as well have been dining alone, he was so intent on me. But Barbara and

Kathryn were happily occupied with their California cuisine.

"I saw no combat myself, being an administrator, but I certainly could see the effects on many of my officers."

"We are beginning to believe that witnesses of trauma, are just as badly affected. Maybe more, because they have to carry on as though there is nothing wrong. The scars are invisible."

"What do you mean?"

"Well, as in your case, seeing your officers wounded, you could experience survivor's guilt at the same time you realize how vulnerable you are. How it could just as easily have been you."

"How then does that pertain to children from dysfunctional family systems?"

I realized he knew the language. He had read the recent spate of self-help literature on the topic.

"Even if the child isn't actually abused or beaten, the threat of it or a violent or unpredictable atmosphere in the home, can produce invisible but lifelong permanent damage."

"What if it is just verbal abuse?"

I knew he must be talking about his own childhood.

"In a way it's worse." I started to get into it and then stopped myself cold. "But I shouldn't be talking shop at dinner. Not good for digestion."

"Do you still take patients?" he continued.

"No. Just pinch hitting for colleagues."

"CC had too many clients at one time," Barbara volunteered.

"Oh, burn-out?" Jeffrey suggested.

"I suppose." I shrugged. It really wasn't burn-out,

more like a moving on, but it was too difficult to try to explain.

"How did you get from the Navy to providing shelter for the homeless, Jeffrey?" Barbara chimed in.

"I guess it's in the genes. My father worked for United Caring for years. I grew up with it. Sort of a modern day Robin Hood, taking from the rich and giving to the poor."

Kathryn laughed gleefully. "Is that what we're doing? I should include that concept in my campaign material."

"You might want to phrase it a bit more tactfully." Jeffrey favored her with a rare smile.

"Does Phyllis think it's okay for you to be riding the campaign trail?" Barbara asked. "Seems like a lot of excitement."

"Yes, indeed. Just what the doctor ordered. Enough excitement to get me revved back up. I'm tired of living so carefully. I'm going to have me a fling and go out in a blaze of glory."

I checked the level of wine in Kathryn's glass and decided her talk was not all alcohol induced.

"Just what did Phyllis say?" I asked. "Did she give you a go ahead?"

"I haven't told her yet. But don't worry, I will. Isn't this lamb just marvelous?"

"Yes. I'd like to get the ingredients for this sauce. It's very good," Jeffrey added.

I decided not to persist in questioning Kathryn. Who was to say which was better. To slowly fade away or go out in a brilliant flash? I had to admire Kathryn's spunk. And even if it turned out to be expensive, the price tag of her property, who was to say what it was worth. How much should it cost to be a chairman of the board?

"Did you enjoy La Jolla? I understand you attended a conference there recently," Jeffrey asked Barbara.

"Yes indeed. At least the hotel was lovely. You know how it is when you are at a conference, you don't do much else." She glanced at me in desperation. I knew she was worried about where this was going and whether we should let on that I had been checking up on him.

"Where did you stay?" Jeffrey casually asked.

"The Valencia."

"Ah, yes. Very nice." He turned to me very deliberately. "And you, Ms. Scott, were you able to find something to do to entertain yourself?"

I looked him straight in the eye, deciding I didn't have a thing to be ashamed of in checking up on him and not caring whether he knew or not.

"Yes. San Diego is still a wonderful area. But people drive too fast. Very scary," I spoke right up.

Jeffrey returned a direct gaze. "Yes, especially if you don't know where you are going."

I heard his warning, subtle but unmistakable.

"Sometimes those are the most interesting journeys." I parried back, my nerve ends tingling with the certainty that Jeffrey knew I'd been snooping.

Chapter 16

It was the second week in December. Clients' emotional states were intensified around the holidays and the work was not easy.

I swung my arms and shook my shoulders to get rid of the tension that had built up around the back of my neck. It was unsettling to think of all of the clients who'd come to transfer unresolved anger on me. I knew better than to take it personally but sometimes it was overwhelming.

On Saturday after a Cream of Wheat breakfast with Barb, I attacked the rose bushes with pruning shears. It was great therapy. Absorbing to have to concentrate on which branches to remove and satisfying when the decision was made and I got to whack it off. Discharging, I called it. Releasing all the negative emotions I'd stored up over the week.

"Here you are. How charming you look." It was Jennifer and she was referring to my straw hat, I'm sure as my process was certainly not charming.

"Hi there, Jennifer. How's the artwork coming?" I stopped to sit on the porch stoop with her. Her hair was a normal color but moussed up in wet spirals.

"Great. I'm having a show in San Luis. Hope you and Barb can come see it."

"Sure we will. When is it?" I removed my hat since I was now in the shade.

"January 2. I'm so excited."

"Of course you are. It's wonderful for you to have an exhibition." Her soft sculptures sold well in the shops but this was recognition of her as an artist.

She shifted her position, settling in beside me. "How do you think Auntie is doing?"

"Very well. All things considered." I was feeling a bit sensitive about Kathryn. Here Jennifer had assigned me a caretaking task and I had botched it. Of course, I shouldn't have accepted the job in the first place. It really wasn't any of my business.

"I know you did the best you could, CC. But I'm still worried. She's getting in deeper and deeper."

"Oh, on the board of directors?"

"Right. No telling what else Mr. Slick will talk her out of."

"I have been making inquiries in San Diego where he was previously the director. So far he looks legitimate." I saw no point in alarming her until something substantial proved otherwise.

"Do you think she's okay for this election business, though?"

"If Phyllis says it's all right, it seems okay to me."

"She's awfully important to me." Jennifer picked up a stick and scratched in the dirt between flagstones.

"I know." I patted her arm. Jennifer's parents had

both been killed in an auto accident when she was twelve years old.

"I don't know what I'd do if something happened to her."

I suspected she would have to work through the loss of her parents when Kathryn died. Grief was often multiple.

"We're pretty attached to her, too. I miss Phil," I confessed. I had taken for granted how special exchanging veggies and talk over the fence had been. Kathryn was not a gardener. She saw the yard as a chore to be gotten through.

"I'm worried that he'll find out how much more she has. Try to marry her then bump her off to get it."

"I think she is more perceptive of him that that. She knows what she is doing."

"I hope so," Jennifer sighed. "Do you think I'm crazy for worrying about her so?"

"Not at all. I don't like Randall, either. He doesn't feel right to me."

"Thank you, CC. It really helps to talk to you. Jake thinks I'm overly concerned about her."

In a way it helped me to talk to her, too, and have my suspicions confirmed. But I had to wonder if I had selected him as a scapegoat for my own deeper anxieties.

Chapter 17

I waved the grocery list at Barbara who was in the study grading student compositions.

"As long as your popcorn and ice cream are on it," she said with a smile, indulgently teasing me.

"At least they have some food value," I defended. When Barbara did indulge her urge to snack, it was cookies or cakes. None of this healthful stuff for her.

"How about Petrale sole for dinner?" She looked hopeful.

"Are you cooking?" I liked her sole almondine a lot.

"If you trek to the store, the least I can do is cook."

"You have yourself an agreement." I smiled at her. It was truly special, never mind how sappy, to be engaged in the simplest of household concerns with the person you loved.

I checked around the kitchen again for any other needed items, and decided to bake bread when I got back. It was a recent avocation. Not only was homemade superior to what you could buy, the making of it brought added pleasures. I enjoyed the sensuousness of kneading the dough, the ritual of punching it down and waiting for it to rise again, making a connection to all women through all time who make bread. And on cold winter days, the warmth of the oven and the smell of the baking bread brought a sense of well-being no store bought package could contain.

It was raining a cold dreary drizzle. I grabbed my warmest jacket and stepped off the back porch into our adjoining garage.

The automatic door opener strained in mechanical feebleness. I suspected the door was too heavy for the motor, but as long as it continued to work, I couldn't see going to the expense of a new one.

I headed down our country road over the bridge spanning a nearby creek. The rain was transforming the landscape. Giant live oaks dripped diamonds from their leaves. Maple skeletons gleamed silver. I punched a tape button for Kitaro which poured forth from the four corners of the car.

Synthesized percussion boomed out in Kitaro's homage to Mount Fuji.

Suddenly the car lurched and skidded into a spin. I wrestled with the wheel, trying to go opposite the direction of the spin. I knew I musn't go over the bridge.

To my amazement, the car came to a stop right in the middle of the span, avoiding a crash into the rail or over the edge. I got out of the car, my knees wobbling, hanging onto the door to steady myself. A bluejay flew out of the scrub oaks, scolding me for disrupting the peace.

Must have been a patch of ice. I examined the road. There was no black ice. No ice at all on the bridge. Just the drizzle. I looked at the car. The right rear tire was flat. It was a new tire with plenty of tread. Must have picked up a nail or something.

I looked over the bridge rail down into the stream rushing by underneath some fifteen feet, shuddering to think of the damage to the car, or me, had I skidded through the railing.

No one was in sight. People were not about at this time of the day. Most had already gone to work or their appointments. I decided to get the car out of the middle of the road.

It wouldn't start. "Shock. An effect of trauma," I said out loud. When I tried a second time, the engine turned over. I eased the wobbling machinery off the bridge to the side of the road where there was a shoulder.

The tire was ruined now but I didn't care. I'd never trust it again anyway, even if it were repaired. Irrational displacement to inanimate object, I counseled myself.

I decided to go back to our house and call the auto club. A real butch would change her own tire, I thought. But not in the rain in good clothes, my femme argued back. It's so unnecessary. I didn't like to pump my own gas, either. Besides, why pay your membership dues year after year if you never use it.

A flash of light caught my attention and disappeared. I looked around, wishing I had the binoculars. Hair prickled on the back of my neck. Something was there.

I walked toward the direction of the flash. At a clump of trees by the stream, I found footprints in the mud on the bank. Someone fishing for steelhead. The flash was probably a hook caught in a tree and the light happened to catch it just right.

Then I spotted a spent shell on the ground. Another 30-06, I'll bet. I pocketed the shell, just as the sound of a car starting up came through the trees. I ran towards the road. If only I could see that car and find out who it was. I took a shortcut up the hill, huffing and puffing, lungs straining to catch air. The car was gone, but I knew someone had been there.

Chapter 18

I walked on home, putting my jangled nerves and jumbled thoughts on freeze. A typical trauma reaction, I noted. Barbara drove me back to the bridge to wait for the mechanic, a boy actually, who changed the tire, putting on the spare.

There was a definite puncture in the tire.

"What was it?" I asked.

He looked at the tire then held it up and shook it.

"Something's in there. You'll have to take it to a station."

I nodded. I knew what it was, all right, but I didn't want to tell Barbara and worry her.

"I'll take care of it later. I just want to get to the store for now."

However, I did go to a station and wait while another young man sullenly put the wheel on the rack and took off its casing, curving the tire iron around in an efficient arc.

A piece of metal fell to the ground, very much like the one I found in the deer.

"Someone's been using your tires for target practice." The boy took a sudden interest, hitching his greasy levis up over his skinny hips.

I busied myself picking out a new tire, supervising its changing and returning the spare back to its place under the carpet in the trunk.

Only when the mechanic finished and I scooted back into the car, did I allow myself to feel the trembling. I concentrated on my breathing. Taking the air in deeply, letting it out slowly.

It couldn't be a coincidence that it was the same caliber of shell found in the deer. There was another sniper out there and it wasn't Jasper Willard, I was sure. I would stake my professional reputation on that.

I couldn't rule out completely the idea that it was a personal vendetta against me. Perhaps some other client regretted a confidence, afraid it might be held against them in some imaginary court of conscience. Perhaps someone stuck in their transference. Lord knows how many of those there could be.

Pulling myself together, I decided to go to the

market. After all, we still had to eat. I walked the aisles, mechanically marking the items off my list, as I mulled over the problem of what to tell Barbara. I didn't want to alarm her, yet neither did I want to lie.

"What was it?" Barbara asked as we put away the groceries.

"A piece of metal."

"Did you keep it?"

"Yes." I bent over into the refrigerator, putting vegetables into the proper bins.

"Well, where is it?" She was getting suspicious.

I pulled it out of my jacket pocket and handed it over.

"Looks like the same one that killed the deer."

"Yes. But I know it wasn't the client." I tidied up the cupboards as she stowed away some canned goods.

"How can you be so sure? This is getting a little too close for comfort. You could have been hurt." Barbara was getting hot. "I insist that you tell Blakely and Theresa, or I will."

I felt my face flush, hotly. "Please don't. There is no real indication of wrong doing here."

"I suppose you're even going to say this could be yet a third sniper." Barbara was sarcastic.

"That is a possibility that can't be ruled out. This is country and there are a lot of people around here with guns."

"Will you have Blakely at least check out the calibration to see if this one is from the same rifle."

I was relieved. "Of course. That's a very good idea."

Mollified, Barbara went back to the grocery sacks, folding them up as I emptied them of their contents.

Blakely stopped by several days later. It was getting closer to Christmas, and we were decorating a small live tree we brought in each year from the terrace.

"It's the same rifle, all right." Blakely handed me a copy of the lab report. "30-06."

"What now?" Barbara asked.

He shrugged. "Can't very well do a door-to-door search. Inalienable American right, the right to bear arms. Even if we found the rifle, couldn't prove your tire was shot out on purpose."

I nodded. I could understand his position.

Barbara was not so understanding. "You mean we have to wait until someone is hurt before you can do anything?"

"Yes. Sorry. It's a little like not arresting someone for thinking about robbing a bank. Have to wait till they try to do it."

"And then you probably better catch them in the act if you want the charge to stick." I was being facetious but Blakely was not.

"Yes. Circumstantial evidence is still considered pretty flimsy, although some of the new genetics tests are making up for it."

Later Barbara remarked, "What bothers me is how they knew you would be driving along then."

"That's why I think there is another sniper. Someone is still shooting at random and happened to be there as I drove by."

"I don't know. It gives me the creeps to think that someone might have been watching us." Her shoulders shuddered.

It gave me the creeps, too. I wasn't convinced of my random shooting theory at all.

Chapter 19

The next day was winter sunshine bright, but I was exhausted from the tire shooting. Sheer tension had taken its toll. Barbara drew a light blue envelope from the morning's junk mail stack. She held it up to show me. I squinted at it, still trying to wake up with a cup of coffee.

The return address was Carmel.

I gestured for her to open it. I was not in verbal mode yet. Besides the fatigue, early morning is not my best time. I think this is how my father must have felt most of the time. Dull, disinterested. A bit disgruntled and negative. In short, depressed. An unpleasant state I would not underestimate in others. For me, though, it's usually a temporary state that soon passes. And if I didn't over react, it would soon right itself. I just waited for the more cheerful aspects of the day to unfold themselves. In this particular instance, it was a note from two new friends.

"What does it say?" I found my voice.

"They would like to come visit. Go on the eagle watch."

"Let me see." I reached for the note.

Light blue notepaper with a navy border contained a simple salutation and inquiry as to whether the invitation to go to the lake was still good.

We had dropped a thank-you note in the mail to Guy and Armando after our dinner in Carmel, inviting them to Dos Pueblos to go to Lake San Antonio to see eagles. Weeks had passed without a response, leaving us to believe the men were not interested in cultivating a friendship.

"I thought they found us uninteresting," Barbara confessed.

"The men are changing," I said thinking about the effect of AIDS and gay men's attempts at broadening their areas of recreational interest beyond sex. A sex substitute was the safest sex of all.

We telephoned them to make plans for meeting at the lake the next Saturday, since it was located on the border between our two counties. Then Guy and Armando would follow us home for dinner and an overnight visit.

"I just hope I don't get seasick." Clad in linen slacks with a cashmere cardigan draped over his shoulders, Armando looked like a pleasure seeker from another century.

"You can't get seasick," Guy insisted scornfully. "It's a flat bottom boat and this is a lake. See, no waves."

We all laughed at the familiar routine. Married couples everywhere were not quite as courteous with one another as they were with strangers.

The tour boat put out from ranger headquarters at

the lake. It wasn't a real lake. Engineers plugged up the river with a dam. Thank goodness, the eagles had made good use of it, anyway.

A small flock of folks, elders with canes and binoculars and youngsters with anxious parents trying to control their wild energies, queued up to board the launch. A black-clad photographer set up thousands of dollars worth of equipment in the front of the boat. Barb and I dashed for seats as close to the tripods as we could to study the array of mechanisms. We knew how difficult it was to photograph birds, even big ones like eagles.

Guy Rathborne looked at home on the boat in his Levi 501's and blue and white striped shirt, a sailor costume evoking his seaman days. But Armando appeared to be out of his element.

On the way to the nesting sites, we caught the men up to date on the Jeffrey Randall matter.

"I'm sure he knows I'm checking up on him. He as much as warned me away."

"Threatened you?" Guy asked.

"No. Just a warning. He's very subtle."

We also reported on the sniper and my near mishap on the bridge.

"Maybe there's a connection," Armando said with a frown.

"You mean that Randall could be the second sniper?" I thought this might be a bit too tidy. Too easy. But it was tempting.

"The shootings started before he moved here," I remembered.

"But he could have kept on doing it after your client stopped." Guy made the connection, too.

An idea began to take shape. I would propose it

later when I'd had a chance to ponder it further.

The friendly inland sunshine beamed down on us, forcing me to put on my straw hat, which I hated, but Barbara thought looked fetching. It was a glorious day with lots of eagles, both Bald and Golden.

I waited until after dinner to bring up my notion. We were sitting in front of a cozy fire in the wood stove listening to Vivaldi. The idea began to take on distinct possibilities.

"A lovely day," sighed Armando. "I'll never forget those magnificent eagles. I have never seen Golden eagles before."

"No wonder our forefathers made an eagle the national symbol," Guy added.

"Now that was a wrong turning in the course of history." Barbara was about to warm up to this topic, a bit piqued at his use of a gender word, but I had another agenda and I didn't want us to get side tracked.

"Guy, would you consider going to San Diego and taking that job on a temporary basis just to find out for sure what it is Jeffrey has to hide and why Mildred covered up for him."

Armando leaned forward. "So you agree there is some connection between Jeffrey and your accident."

"I honestly don't know. But pursuing the matter seems to stir things up. I can't just leave it alone."

"I don't know why not," Barbara began but silenced herself at the look I threw her.

Guy was quiet, leaning back on the chintz-covered sofa, pondering my proposal.

"What about the other candidate? The one already in San Diego."

"Oh yes. Matthew Sorens. To tell you the truth, I didn't think of him. It's a lot to ask of a stranger."

A look passed between the two men, with Armando nodding.

Guy sighed. "The reason I'm hesitating is that I've been diagnosed HIV positive. I have to have a lot of medical tests in the next few months. I hadn't been feeling well for some time. Finally, I decided to go for the test. I didn't want to know what I found out."

I nodded. "It must have been hard." A painful stab of awareness made me know how inadequate these words were.

"He doesn't have the stamina to work a full day, anyway," Armando said, worry furrowing his handsome face. "He gets tired and needs to rest. I'd rather he stay home. Travel is exhausting."

"Hell, everything is exhausting," Guy interrupted, grinning. "But that doesn't mean I won't do it. Especially if this Sorens can't."

"So that's why we didn't hear from you," Barbara said, her voice full of feeling.

"Yes. You really go through some emotional changes when you find out you have a life-threatening illness. At first I needed time just to deal with it, accept it, not be angry."

"And find out who your friends are," Armando put in, with a touch of bitterness.

"Not gay friends?" I queried.

"Yes, even our own brothers and sisters have AIDS phobia."

How awful it was. The lonely suffering of stigma. For tuberculosis patients in the twenties. Polio victims in the fifties. Our fear of death making us segregate our dying so we don't have to see it. So we can pretend it isn't really happening.

"But life goes on." Guy leaned near me conspiratorially. "Tell me what you want me to do, Miss Marple."

"You will do it?" I was moved in admiration of his courage.

"Only if your Sorens won't." Guy looked to his partner. "Probably wouldn't be but a few weeks to find out something one way or another."

Armando shook his head. "I'm banking on Sorens. You don't need to be a hero anymore. You've got enough on your plate."

Later that night as we got ready for bed, Barbara said, "It's so senseless. Such a waste of intelligence and talent when they are in their prime."

"An entire generation of elite," I commiserated.

"I almost feel guilty that we aren't at risk."

"Just the luck of the draw," I reminded her. "The way some of the younger lesbians are going, our sisters will be at risk too." The next generation had seemed to rebel against our staid sisterhood and exploded into a sexual revolution.

"Yes, it's funny how it worked out. Sexually, gay men and women have changed places."

"I like our way better." Barbara reached under the covers to pull up my flannel nightgown.

Chapter 20

Asking Matt Sorens to take the job for spying purposes didn't seem to be something I could tackle on the phone. So I flew down to San Diego to talk to him in person, taking the little puddle-jumper flight out of Dos Pueblos and transferring in Los Angeles to the coast commuter an hour later. Flying was more trouble than it was worth, and outrageously expensive for such a short hop, but this way I could meet him at the airport and then turn around and be back home in time for dinner.

"I have already accepted the position," he said. "I haven't been able to find another job and that one kept sticking in my craw. It's just right for me."

"But why didn't you tell me when I called?"

"If there were anything illegal going on, I needed to find out what else you know."

I filled him in on my suspicions of Jeffrey's skimming at CARE and his fast work in putting together the new agency in Dos Pueblos.

"When do you start your new position?"

"This Monday."

I realized something about him had changed. A psychic shift. He was now a take charge guy. He even looked more substantial.

"You're looking well," I said. "Fit."

Instead of a sports jacket, he had on a rugby shirt open at the collar and relaxed canvas trousers. A windbreaker added up to a more muscular persona.

"I've been working out. I felt like such a wimp not finding a job and turning down the CARE job. At least I respect myself again," he added.

And so will others, I thought. At the very least he will be able to put CARE back together again, if what he finds out proves destructive for the agency.

I thanked him sincerely before hurrying through the airport to catch my flight back to Dos Pueblos, via Los Angeles and Santa Maria. More time on the ground than in the air, I grumbled, but knew my mission was successful. We now had a competent ally. I was eager to get home and share the good news with Barbara. It was much better to take action and do something, anything, rather than sit around passively and wait for Jeffrey Randall to make a mistake.

Chapter 21

Neat white-rail fences outlined sections of green alfalfa fields. Black Angus heifers roamed one pasture, while Arabians whinnied about in another.

Although I was positive Jasper Willard told the truth about not shooting live ammunition, I decided to visit him anyway. One of life's less pleasant lessons is that just when I'm the most sure of something, I'm the most likely to be dead wrong.

His address was in the phone book. The Black Cow Ranch. I'd driven by its river pastures many times when taking the scenic route to town through the length of our valley, instead of slipping out the short end of it.

This was not your everyday run-down farm. I could see Jasper off in the distance on a horse, herding Angus calves that were bawling and kicking. He waved at me. An empty stock pen was close to the side of the road where I stood near my car. It was obvious that this was Jasper's destination with the cattle.

There was nothing to do but wait for him. Now that I was mostly retired, waiting was a gift of time, an excuse to watch what was going on around me. To witness, as Annie Dillard would say, the astonishing things around us.

Like many big ranches in the area, the Black Cow was a family operation, with a mixed production of cattle, horses, walnuts, almonds and apples. The idea was that if one crop failed or the market dropped, then another might carry the year.

Another rancher client, one who bought Cadillacs a half dozen at a time, told me the bigger they were, the more in debt they were. Not to be fooled by appearances. He claimed the only difference between himself and the homeless is that his credit was still good at the bank.

And you're still sleeping in a warm house, I had countered.

I looked over the spread. Orchards were pruned and tidied up for the winter. Other than the irrigated pastures near the house and barn, the fields were plowed under, a new green velvet already covering the furrows. Stuffed full of alfalfa, the barn was freshly painted white with red trim, to match the rambling adobe house.

This was not the domain of an unbalanced person, I decided.

After Jasper got the small herd penned up with the help of a younger version of himself, he greeted me, still on his horse, a wiry Appaloosa with white abstract circles painted on its rump.

"Hello, Ms. Scott. This is my son, Russell. What can I do for you?"

Jasper didn't even look surprised to see me.

"Hi, Russell. Looks like a healthy bunch."

"Great calving season," he agreed, smiling.

I turned to Jasper. "I need to talk with you about a private matter."

"Oh, Russell? He's my right hand."

"And your left." The younger man laughed at what was obviously an inside joke.

"Go ahead, Pop. I can handle this." He waved at the calves milling about in the corral, still complaining and kicking up dust.

Jasper nodded and rode his horse toward the white ranch house, indicating for me to follow in my car. He tied the Appaloosa's reins to a rail in front of the house near a water trough. The sculptured branches of a dormant elm promised shade when it was needed in the summer.

The inside of the house was cool. I knew how soothing this could be in the summer when it was ninety degrees outside.

"How about some coffee?"

Jasper was proficient in the kitchen. I decided it was not because he was newly-widowed but because he was that kind of man who would give everything equal attention, whether it was attending to cattle, or fixing breakfast for children.

Only after we had our coffee, sitting at the kitchen table, did he indicate his readiness to listen.

"I think someone else has been shooting up in the valley."

He nodded. "I heard 'em, too."

"How often?"

"Three, maybe four times."

"How many times would you say you did it?"

"Five or six, at least."

Jasper studied his coffee cup. He didn't seem worried. "It was a different gun from mine. Maybe a little bigger caliber. Booms more than cracks like mine," he explained.

"This guy is using live ammunition." I wondered if he realized I still wasn't sure of him.

"That's pretty stupid. In a crowded valley like this."

His indignation seemed genuine.

"That's why I need your help. First of all, could I see your rifle, the one you were using?"

"Sure." Jasper stepped over to a locked gun case and took out a Winchester. I couldn't keep from peering suspiciously at the others.

"None of those have been touched in years," he reassured me.

The gun in his hands was well-oiled and clean.

"How can you tell that this is a 30-30?"

"See this cocking lever here?" he indicated just below the trigger. "It makes for faster action. That's how you can tell it's a 30-30."

"Now could I see the shell, the blanks you were using."

Jasper nodded agreeably and went to a locked chest beside the cabinet, finding the right key on a ring in his pocket.

"Keep things locked up because of the grandkids."

"A good idea," I said.

The blank was a cartridge without a bullet. Inside was its powder, tamped down and sealed with a wax that looked like lipstick.

"May I keep this just for my own education?"

"Of course." His trust of me was unmistakable, but I decided it wouldn't hurt to have Blakely double-check to make sure it could not have been loaded with live ammunition the same as the slugs from the deer or the tire.

"Don't you think the sheriff ought to be looking into this, instead of you?" Jasper seemed to read my mind with his question.

"Well, I have a duty as a therapist to protect your identity and part in these shootings, so it was better for me to check with you myself." I smiled to let him know it was okay. "Besides I know beans about guns, so here was an opportunity to learn something. Also it was a good excuse to come out and see your ranch."

"And see how I am doing?"

I smiled at his astuteness. "And see how you are doing."

"I'm letting the boys do more of the work. I'm learning to take better care of myself. I was so used to Abby doing it. Telling me when to eat, when to go to bed, when to stop working." He grinned good naturedly at his own learned helplessness.

"I've joined up with the disaster corps. If we have an earthquake like the October '89, we'll know what to do. Either of those dams could bust or the nuclear power plant could melt down. Even out here in the middle of this peace and quiet, we're sitting on ecological disasters."

I was reminded that ranchers, often educated at Berkeley and Harvard, were generalists. They had to be able to do everything to keep a ranch working. They were ecologists, veterinarians, engineers and builders.

"A way to be around other people once a week. Sort of my kind of therapy," he explained further.

And psychologists, I added to the list.

"Is there training? Do you have drills?" A disaster corps like this was a splendid idea. It seemed to me that ordinary citizens could do a lot to help ourselves, if we just had an idea of what to do.

"Yep. Twice a month we get lectures and drills over at the National Guard. They're the ones training us."

"How many of you are there?"

"Only ten to a team. But our team is part of a squad. Must be forty of us altogether from all over the county."

I bet some retired football coach had a hand in the organizing.

"Are there any women?" I didn't want to be the only one.

"Sure are. Some of the women are better than the men."

"Must have been an eye opener to some of the men."

"We have a good group, Ms. Scott. Why don't you come to our next orientation lecture?"

"Thank you. I will, Jasper." Perhaps once all this business with the sniper was sorted out, this would be something to engage my interest. I like the idea of not being so dependent on experts, who would not be enough to go around, anyway, in a real disaster.

Chapter 22

My next stop that afternoon was Randall's. A small white frame cottage with blue trim sat at the end of a private road. I could hear Zacky creek rushing by, swollen from recent rain. The house stood under a cluster of bare limbed ash and locust trees, with one Monterey pine a daub of green.

As I'd hoped, no one was home.

I parked in back of the house, out of sight for anyone coming up the drive. Then I went around the side of the house, not much bigger than a cabin, to the front door. It wasn't even locked.

This is too easy. What do I think I'm going to find anyway? At least there are no dogs to contend with.

Sparsely furnished, but tidy and clean, I guessed it was little more than a temporary headquarters. A sofa and easy chair in homespun beige cozied up to a modern airtight wood stove.

Another dark wood-tiered niche held the electronic marvels, the television, compact disc and video.

The room was masculine and unadorned except for a Matisse print. I wondered if it had already been here. Randall didn't seem to be the fanciful type. Perhaps someone gave it to him. Mildred came to mind. Modern and flashy.

A darkened pine bookcase held a few books; some mysteries, a book on identifying mushrooms, a dictionary, Peter's *Search for Excellence.*

Nothing unusual.

Nothing unusual, except a piece of paper sticking up from the book on excellence. It was a newspaper clipping, old and yellowed. An article about a deer hunter who accidentally bled to death in the Yolla Bolly mountains in Northern California.

Mark Randall, a charity fundraiser. He had to be Jeffrey's father. I remembered his questions at dinner at the hotel that night, asking about verbal abuse of a child.

I scanned the article. His father must have been an important man to get so much newspaper space. Jeffrey was mentioned as a survivor at the end. Eighteen years old. In the Marines. But I thought he was in the Navy. It was confusing. I put the clipping back where it had been and returned the book to the shelf. This wasn't exactly what I was after.

I entered the bedroom, stealthily, hardly daring to breathe. It was one thing to enter a person's unlocked house, but it was quite another to go into a man's bedroom. My first impression was of extreme neatness. It looked like a motel room with nothing personal in it. One bed, one dresser, one chair and a wood valet, presently empty, on top of the dresser.

Definitely a single man's resting place. I put aside a feeling of guilt that I ought not to be prying in someone else's private space. After all, I've been probing people's private spaces for years. So what was one more bedroom.

In the closet the clothes glistened in plastic bags, fresh from the cleaners. I could smell the chemicals. It looked like he'd even had his cotton shirts and pants done at the laundry.

A rifle lurked in the back of the closet.

I pushed the clothes to one side to get a better look at it. I knew not to touch it.

Similar to the gun Jasper showed me, but a bit longer with darker metal, the wood stock looked like it was sculpted from one piece. I knew it had to be the 30-06. I put the clothes back like they were.

There's nothing like a little success to give me courage. I checked out the dresser next. The top right hand drawer contained neatly rolled up sox, belts, and gloves. The left held a jewelry chest and a cardboard box of shells. Thirty-ought six was printed in black block letters on its top.

I opened the box. Bullets sat upright in their cases in two rows. Seven cartridges were missing from the carton. I took out a shell and put it in my pocket.

The sound of a car crunching on the gravel was distant, but distinct. My heart started jack hammering.

Chapter 23

Quickly, I replaced the cover of the box and put it back where I found it. Then I dashed around the side of the house, panting and puffing, panicky that I wouldn't get to the car before Randall. I made it and jumped in the car, whacking my knee against the door jamb. I started the engine and was turning around to come back out when Jeffrey Randall's car appeared in the drive.

The Mercedes stopped in front of me, deliberately blocking my way.

"Well, I almost missed you," I said lamely.

"To what do I owe the pleasure of your company?" His voice was hard.

"I was just out for a drive." I concentrated on keeping my breathlessness from showing. "I remembered you'd said you lived out here. Thought I'd see if you were home."

Jeffrey got out of his car and came to my window, peering inside the car. "It was lucky that I just happened to come home early today."

I looked at my watch. It was four o'clock. "I didn't even know what time it was. Now that I'm not regularly employed anymore, I forget that other people keep schedules." I smiled as winningly as I could, remembering the chimp research that indicated smiling evolved to ward off aggression.

"Well, now that you're here. Why don't you come in for something to drink. Some coffee."

He apparently remembered from our dinner out that we didn't drink alcohol. Although his invitation was correct and courteous, his tone of voice was not. He looked menacing, his face dark with displeasure. I felt a stab of fear. Coming out here alone had not been a very good idea.

I had my evidence, the 30-06 cartridge, and I should have wanted to get the hell out of there. But the curiosity of the therapist prevailed. What was it exactly that had happened on that hunting trip, for one, and what was the extend of Jeffrey's psychic scarring? How had it manifested itself?

"All right, but just a cold drink, a soda if you have it. I don't have much time. It's my turn to cook dinner tonight." I babbled nervously.

He nodded and returned to his Mercedes to park it beside my car, leaving the drive clear. It was not too late to make a run for it, but perversely, I followed him into the cabin.

"I've been meaning to ask you some questions," he began, handing me a can of coke and a glass and sitting down in the easy chair, leaving the sofa for me.

"Yes?" I hardly dared to speak.

"You were saying a child can be permanently damaged by verbal or emotional abuse?"

"Yes. In a way it's worse, because the adult child doesn't see that there was any obvious harm to them."

"Invisible scars," he repeated thoughtfully.

I held my tongue. Actually, they were not so invisible. The trauma would work itself out in ways that were very apparent—compulsions, addictions, eating disorders, asocial acts.

"My father was an alcoholic." Jeffrey stopped cold at his disclosure, waiting for a response.

"Mine was depressed. Very similar dynamics," I offered.

He nodded. "He died in a hunting accident. It was my fault."

This caught me by surprise. "But how? You were..." I held my tongue.

"I was eighteen, in the Marines. I joined the Navy after that hitch," he explained. "He talked me into going hunting when I was on leave. I couldn't say no. He was a bully—demanding and arrogant. People did want he wanted." Jeffrey's speech was terse, without feeling.

It was classic egocentricity of the alcoholic, all right, the alcohol destroying awareness of other people's feelings.

"Yes, that's an effect of the alcohol," I said.

"I hated him." Suddenly, Jeffrey was eighteen again and reliving what happened.

"He was dressing out the deer, a buck. I was making a sled with branches to take it out of a ravine. We were in snow a half mile from the truck in the mountains. Rugged country.

"The knife slipped. He wasn't wearing gloves. Stabbed himself in the gut," Jeffrey described without inflection, without feeling. No *affect* as we say.

"I had to go for help. He was gone when I got back with the medics."

"It wasn't your fault, Jeffrey," I said softly.

He looked at me sharply, as though he'd just come out of a trance.

"Sure, it was. But he deserved to die."

Cold prickles ran up my spine. It was going to take a lot more than one accidental encounter with a therapist to resolve this conflict. I remembered this man was my nemesis and was probably dangerous.

"I think I'd better go. Thank you for the coke." I headed for the door.

"Next time, you might want to call," he said carefully. He was giving me warning. "Kathryn has my number."

"Yes, thank you, I will." I chose to treat it like a polite invitation, my mind blanking out with relief.

I stepped on the gas, but eased out, unwilling to spray gravel and reveal how eager I was to get out of there. The fear was quickly replaced with elation, leaving me to marvel at what a fine line there could be between the two.

As interesting as Jeffrey's disclosures were, the real prize was the 30-06 shell, now nestled in my pocket.

Chapter 24

My elation over the discovery of Randall's rifle and shells was short-lived. I couldn't very well reveal to either Barbara or Blakely how I had come by such information. Neither would approve of my sneaking into his house like that. Blakely, because it is breaking and entering. Well, entering. At least I didn't break in. And Barbara because she would be very worried that I would resort to such drastic measures.

I regretted so much secrecy. Perhaps doing therapy for so many years has over-developed my private side. My bias, by training and experience, is that the happiest and most well adjusted of humans seem to be quite open and freely self-disclosing. Being well adjusted can be a terrible price to pay for not being authentic, however. And happiness is merely the fleetingest of moments, anyway.

An unorthodox life style could also cultivate a clandestine nature. Learning to disclose as little as possible until I'm sure of being on secure ground with another person is an essential survival skill.

But what I can do is telephone Matt Sorens in San Diego and see if he has learned anything yet from his inside position as the new director. I would be content with anything that might reveal Jeffrey Randall was not the upright citizen he seemed to be.

"So far, I can't see a thing out of order. The paperwork is impeccable. The files are clean. Of course, I've only been here one week. Something else could turn up."

"Is Mildred still the secretary?"

"Yes, but we're negotiating a golden parachute."

"She wants to leave?" I raised an eyebrow at Barbara across the room in our study. She had just turned her attention from the bird feeder outside the window where titmice were snatching their booty of safflower seeds and soaring away.

"I'd rather not have a secretary. It's a job category that exploits women. With today's E Mail and fax machines, people don't really need them, anymore. And we're compensating her handsomely for her years of service." Matt sounded confident, sure of himself.

"That's a refreshing point of view, coming from a man." I was sincere in my appreciation.

Matt chuckled. "Besides, she wants to do things the way Randall did them. Hard for her to make the transition." His voice faded on the telephone.

"She might just be the reason you can't find any evidence of funny business. Her daughter is an attorney," I remembered to tell him.

"Just a minute. Let me make sure this line is clear."

There was a silence, a clicking noise and then a dial tone indicating a disconnect.

I juggled the receiver. "Hello, Matt? Are you there?" He was obviously not there. I hung up the phone.

"I guess he'll call back. I suspect the problem was on his end," I explained to Barbara.

"Mildred," she replied.

"Could be. Does seem to be quite a coincidence, doesn't it?"

"No wonder she wants to leave, with Matt prying around." Barbara smiled. "Suggests a guilty conscience to me."

"Yes, indeed. I think we're on to something. Perhaps the weak link."

The phone rang. Matt said it was an accidental disconnect.

"Please be careful, Matt. I don't trust Mildred."

"Thank you for your concern, CC. But I'm in the driver's seat now."

"Even the best driver can get the wrong directions."

I didn't want him to underestimate the capability of someone like Mildred.

"Would you like me to send you what I have?" Matt changed the subject.

"Sure. What did you find?"

"I started to tell you before we were disconnected, I do have all the agency records of the board members who made bequests to CARE."

"And what about their death certificates, coroner's reports, autopsies?" I could hear how grisly this sounded.

Matt was silent for a moment. "So that's what you suspect. Okay. I can do that. Might take a little time. I'll have to get someone else to do it for us. A private investigator, if that's okay with you."

I liked his use of the pronoun, us, and his taking the initiative on how to handle his end.

The files arrived two days later by parcel service, the familiar brown van pulling away, the driver Louisa waving her arm out the window.

Five packets contained data on four women and one man.

"So he doesn't prey solely on women," I said to Barb.

"Retired military. Like Randall. Maybe he was a superior officer when they were in the Navy," she said as she got into the spirit of our inquiry.

The four women were all, variously, over seventy and widowed, except one, a retired librarian.

"Penelope Oberland. Took over her husband's company, when he died of a heart attack. Electronic components." I read aloud from a biography sheet.

"Drusila Sanderson. President of her family firm. Corpair Aviation. A private charter flight company." Barbara read from another.

"Here's a good one." I had to smile at my discovery. "Anne Roberts Turgot. Founding partner of Deep Divers Unlimited. She kept her family name ahead of her time."

"You never hear about women like these in the media," complained Barbara.

"Just not as ridiculous as Zsa-Zsa or Leona throwing tantrums."

"Maybe the previous generation was underestimated," Barbara mused.

"Or maybe we don't come into our full power until we are in our sixties and seventies."

"Who is the fourth woman?"

"Charlotte Buchanan. Never married. Lived with another librarian."

"How can you tell?" Barbara peered over my shoulder.

I pointed to the emergency contact section. A woman's name was listed. Emily Macias, with the phone number indicated to be the San Diego Public Library.

"Looks like a *sister* to me."

"Maybe. Not all women who live together are lesbians."

"Well, look who's not leaping to conclusions." Barbara was good natured, as always.

Chapter 25

Matt's cover letter stated that the coroner's reports on the details of their deaths would be forwarded as soon as he could acquire them. That it might take a week or two.

"These files are certainly impressive," Barbara observed, leafing through the papers. "Are you sure you aren't chasing up a dead end?"

I ignored her skepticism.

In addition to the biographical sketches, each board member's file contained an agreement of terms of office, a grant deed and a deed of trust. The financial records of each file were neatly labeled and detailed.

"Looks like Randall netted about $50,000 on each transaction." I compared the amounts, ranging from a low of $32,000 to a high of $74,000.

"Doesn't seem like an unreasonable amount." Barbara frowned at the neat figures.

"Perhaps not for most people." But I had seen from my parent's situation, how a thirty-five year mortgage taken out in the fifties meant mortgages one fifth the amount their neighbors paid. They were equity rich and could get reverse mortgages to help them out with unexpected expenses. It was one of the few ways seniors could survive on small social security payments and shrinking pension funds.

"Our equity would be closer to two hundred when we reach their age." I calculated the worth of our property and compared it to the San Diego real estate market. The acreage, rebuilt house and barn would be paid off by the time we were in our seventies.

"What are you saying?" Barbara was attentive.

"I'll bet there was more equity than what came to the agency."

"You think Randall skimmed some?"

"Skimmed a lot. He must have. He must have a lot to cover up," I conjectured.

Barbara looked at me sharply. "Is there something you're not telling me?"

"No, no. Just intuition, and now the arithmetic to back it up."

"There was no double-dealing in this paperwork." Barbara indicated the meticulous documentation.

"Too careful," I argued. "Look at this." I went to my desk to bring out our own mortgage papers and handed them to her.

"Not as neat," Barbara conceded.

"Ours are a mess."

Mistakes, typographical errors, actually, were sprinkled throughout the papers, with our initials approving the corrections. The sight of those scrawls whipped me into a time warp. They had been executed in an emotional state akin to getting married. Afterall, buying a home is the most important transaction most people will make. And for gays and lesbians, often the sole legal instrument for executing a binding contract on their relationship.

Fifteen years ago, after sharing rentals for over five years, we mulled over various living together agreements and settled on a fifty-fifty plan. We each mustered up half of the down payment. Me, with a loan from mother that I've paid back over the years; Barbara, by borrowing against a life insurance policy she'd had since a teenager.

Although locked into debt together and committed to the mortgage payments as joint tenants, neither did we want to make a prison, so we hammered out the logistics for a breakup.

"Here we are planning our divorce even before we've gotten married," Barbara had complained.

"I know it seems cold and calculating, but spelled out like this, we will avoid hard feelings in the future."

I couldn't help but see with couples I counseled that it was community property that gave people the most fits. I couldn't count how many times a couple sat in my office complaining about the other partner's spending habits. When I would propose separate finances with individual bank accounts, they would be astounded at the simplicity of the solution. In cases where the man made more money than the woman, which was still all too frequently the case, I suggested proportionate shares. And I always held out for the woman having her own money, unaccountable to her partner.

Neither of us had wanted to emulate these troublesome features of the heterosexual union. As far as domestic chores were concerned, fifty-fifty was also the prevailing principle. If one cooked, the other washed up. And if we were both uninspired, we went out to a nice restaurant.

"Why don't you have our accountant look at these papers? Maybe she could see something we can't."

Barbara brought me back to the present. I had to admit executing a living trust is not the same thing as our house purchase, but the absence of any human error in the typographical perfection raised my suspicions.

"Let's wait and see what else Matt can find out." Hard evidence. Something concrete, like the shell from Randall's cottage, was what I wanted.

Chapter 27

Shelterworks was popular the minute they'd opened the doors. At this time last year the police had routed the homeless out of the creekside thickets in San Luis. Many citizens thought it a poor way to treat the homeless at Christmas time when temperatures were in the twenties.

"This is a good program for women because they provide child care," I was explaining to Vera when Randall appeared at her office door. He seemed annoyed.

"Something has come up. I have to leave for the day."

He nodded at me. "Sorry to interrupt."

"Oh, I'm sorry. Is there anything I can do?" Vera immediately responded.

This seemed like a dejâ vu to me. A replay.

"No. Just something personal. But thank you. I'll see you tomorrow."

I wrapped up my discussion with Vera. It was close to ten o'clock anyway. Then I raced to the bank. Sure enough. Randall was just pulling out. Again I followed him.

Driving the twenty or so miles to San Luis was a pleasant commute over an elevation that began with bucolic pastures and lifted to a craggy cliff showing off a panoramic ocean fifteen miles away. But I was intent on keeping the Mercedes in sight without him seeing me.

This time he took the Madrone off-ramp on the south side of town and pulled into the parking lot of the Madrone Inn. It's a garish purple landmark blighting the scenery on highway 101 that's become a honeymoon destination and tourist stop.

Inside, he met Mildred in the restaurant, just as I suspected. I took a table behind a ponderous wood carving hoping they wouldn't see me yet I would be able to hear them.

"This place is absolutely wild. Almost worth the drive." I heard her say. A local farmer had made good and built a restaurant and hotel on a fantasy scale. Christmas decorations adorned every square inch of the restaurant including a human-sized doll swinging back and forth in a winter tableau.

"You should see the rooms." I heard Jeffrey say.

"I've heard about them. All done on different themes. Elaborate. Was it a truck drivers' stop originally?"

I peered around my pillar to see Mildred checking the contents of the envelope and putting it in her purse with a flash of smile for Jeffrey.

"Truck drivers have better taste." It was strange to hear him make jokes. He was in good humor for being blackmailed.

They ordered brunch. By now it was eleven o'clock. I asked for toast. I was too excited to eat.

Mildred spoke *sotto voce*, almost whispering, her voice was so quiet.

"The new director is snooping around. He's been talking on the phone with that psychologist friend of yours. And I saw a package go ..." her voice disappeared in some room noise.

"Do you know what files?" Jeffrey's voice came back in, sharp.

"No. He's very secretive." There was silence. I risked peering around the sculpture again, a large deer it was, to see if they were still there.

"In fact, I'm being let go. He claims he doesn't need a secretary."

"What are you going to do?" he asked.

"Not me. We, Jeffrey. We're in this together. We need to make a plan."

"My dear, I don't think we should discuss this any further in a public place. I took the liberty of engaging a room here to which we can adjourn after our lunch."

He was smooth, all right.

"You devil, you. I don't know that I can stay long," she hedged, but her delight was unmistakable.

So that's why he would be gone for the rest of the day. A little blackmail, for what I wondered. A little hanky panky to keep the alliance bonded. Two of a kind, I reckoned.

Chapter 28

It was over a week later when the results of that alliance made themselves known. Matt's voice was sharp on the telephone.

"I've been ill with the flu, or what I thought was the flu, until I got a warning letter in the mail."

"What does it say?" I was pleased. Things were definitely starting to happen.

"'Next time it won't seem like just the flu.'"

"You mean that you were poisoned?" My elation faded. This was much more than I'd bargained for.

"The note is written with letters cut out from magazines and states, *Next time it won't seem like the flu.*"

"When did you become ill?" I made a note of the word, flu, on the notepad by the kitchen telephone.

"Two days ago. It lasted about twenty-four hours. I'm afraid it's too late to do any chemical testing."

"I'm really sorry, Matt. I should have told you

sooner that Mildred and Randall met in San Luis last week." The hair on the back of my neck prickled as I made the connection.

"Probably wouldn't have changed anything. It could be that I really did have the flu, and someone decided to capitalize on it with a threat."

"Yes, that's a possibility I didn't think of."

"Mildred did have an opportunity. She brought me coffee. She could have put something in it," he countered.

"How is flu spelled?" I remembered to ask.

"F-L-U," he answered. "And the postmark is Los Angeles."

"She could have driven to Los Angeles to mail the note." I shifted the telephone to hear his voice better. I was aware that Barbara had come into the kitchen, probably drawn to the serious tone in our discussion.

"Yes, but why did you ask about the spelling?" Matt's voice rose in puzzlement.

"Most people spell it like a chimney flue with an 'E' on the end. As a secretary, Mildred is a good speller. And her daughter, the lawyer, would spell it right, too." I was just thinking out loud.

"Maybe you better take this threat very seriously, Matt, and lay off for now." I looked at Barbara who nodded at the gist of it.

"Oh, no. Not now. Now I'm angry. If she really poisoned me with something, I intend to prosecute her. And if she and Randall had anything to do with those board members' deaths, I want to see them hang for it."

"I don't like this, Matt. It could be dangerous."

"I'll be careful, CC. And she damn well won't get another chance at me. Besides, I've hired an investigator and she should have a preliminary report to me by the end of this week."

It did not escape my attention that the investigator he hired was of the female gender. Matt continued to rise in my reckoning.

"When is Mildred's last day at work?"

"This Friday. I probably won't go in until then. Oswald can run things without me. So far, I'm just a figurehead."

"Well, please be careful. It does look like we're getting somewhere. People are resorting to drastic measures." I had to allow a little bit of gloating.

"Don't worry about me. Better watch things on your end." Matt was prescient.

The other shoe fell several days later when Saturday's mail arrived.

"I don't understand this. It's a mistake." Barbara held up a letter from the district superintendent on school board stationary.

"What is it?" I was atop a ladder pruning an apple tree. I came right down. Several Western Bluebirds flew up in alarm at my sudden descent. It was a brilliantly clear day with marshmallow clouds in a deep blue sky.

"They say my credential is not up to date. I've been dropped as a substitute teacher."

I looked at the letter. It certainly seemed authentic.

"Let's go inside and see if we can figure this out." I put my arm around her to comfort her. I knew this was a big shock. Barbara always minded her P's and Q's.

"Maybe it's a mistake. A clerical error."

I put on the kettle for tea, letting the offending

letter sit in the middle of the kitchen table.

Over our tea, a bracing sassafras, I proposed calling the superintendent to see if it was actually a board decision, or a mistake.

Barbara found his home number in the telephone book and dialed the number.

"Doctor Musselman? This is Barbara Bettencourt, a substitute teacher in the Dos Pueblos district. I've received a letter dropping me from the rolls."

I watched her face crumble as she listened to the voice on the other end of the instrument.

"I see. Is the decision irrevocable?" she motioned for me to go into the study and listen on the extension.

"So you see, Ms. Bettencourt, my hands are tied by the decisions of the board. It's meant to be more egalitarian with a concensus process. The decision is the conscience of the community via its representatives."

"Then you are saying that even if I supply a duplicate record proving my updating, the board has already found me unfit as a role model for children."

"This is off the record, you understand. I didn't like it, myself. But the citizens believed your, ah, unorthodox lifestyle called into question your suitability as a teacher of our young. Parents are always afraid someone will proselytize their children. Especially today with so much child abuse going on, we have to have our teachers be impeccable."

"Being gay or lesbian does not mean one is a sexual offender, Doctor Musselman."

"I know that, Barbara, but this is a kind of redneck district. People lump sexual deviants and sexual offenders together."

His sexism was revealed in addressing Barb by her

first name. Language was an amazing thing. By using the phrase sexual deviants, we both knew the superintendent was a hypocrite. His prejudice was blatantly obvious. He did not know that homosexuality is no more deviant than heterosexuality; that the two extremes were distorted mirror images of each other.

"This will not be the end of this," Barbara vowed.

"I'm sorry you want to make trouble. It will only escalate your problems." There was warning in his voice.

Barbara hung up the telephone.

"I didn't trust myself to say another word," she reported when I came back into the kitchen.

"I'm sorry. That's rotten. I'd forgotten that kind of mentality could still exist."

"It just got more polite." Barbara wadded up the letter and threw it across the room.

"Seems to me we need a good attorney. How about Dolly Han?" I remembered a feminist lawyer who specialized in discrimination cases.

"Can we afford her now that I'm not working, CC?"

"Can't afford not to. And it's not your fault this happened. It's mine. Don't you see? This reaction means we must be getting on to something big. Besides you'll get back pay and special damages."

I got out my address book to find someone who might know where Dolly was these days. This tactic of attacking Barbara was hitting below the belt and I wanted immediate retaliation.

Over twenty years ago, Dolly had won a case against a school board in Pasadena for a teacher investigated by the FBI. The irony was the investigation had been totally unnecessary. While in the Navy, the teacher had applied for officer candidacy some three years prior. When the FBI got around to evaluating her suitability as an officer, she wasn't even in the Navy, anymore. The FBI had gleefully accepted an outdated case just to give its boys some practice. And the bureau was under the dictatorship of the homophobic Hoover, himself a closet case. Small wonder there had been a civil rights explosion in the sixties against such mindless oppression.

Dolly had persuaded a jury that the teacher should have her job reinstated with back pay and special damages for harassment, particularly because the agents had come to the woman's fifth grade classroom and arrested her with handcuffs in front of her frightened students. The teacher had tried to salvage a civics lesson out of it.

"How do you suppose Jeffrey got through to the school board?" I asked Barbara.

"Maybe he didn't. Maybe he had nothing to do with it."

Barbara stared at me. I wondered what she was thinking.

"But I heard them," I protested.

"You heard them what? That Mildred and Jeffrey are continuing to have a relationship?"

Barb just didn't see the menace that Matt and I did.

Several calls later, I was successful. I outlined the situation to Dolly, now headquartered in San Francisco.

"We have about a fifty-fifty chance of prevailing in civil discrimination suits these days."

"Are you trying to discourage us?" I was surprised.

"No. Just being realistic. The climate is less

tolerant of gay and lesbian issues because of AIDS."

"All the more reason we need to fight back." Now I was aroused.

We made an immediate appointment for a strategy planning session in San Francisco at Dolly's office.

"Even if we lose, we'll make a heck of a ruckus and cause things to be very uncomfortable for the school board and Mr. Randall," I promised Barbara.

Chapter 29

"Can we talk for a minute, CC?" Jennifer caught me in the kitchen putting more chocolate chip cookies and canapes out for our guests. It was the night before Christmas eve when we took our turn hosting a neighborhood gathering.

She set to helping me arrange the trays. She was excited, all breathless and pink-cheeked. *Jingle Bells* was being sung in the living room in a reasonable rendition.

"How about in the morning?" I was quite distracted. Kathryn had brought Jeffrey Randall into our home, presuming, with no information to the contrary, that he was welcome. It was my own fault. We never said a word to indicate our suspicion of him. In fact, we had protected Kathryn from knowing of my investigative efforts. I knew now that that could have been a mistake. Neither could I discuss it with Jennifer and worry her unduly or prematurely. But Jennifer's mind was elsewhere.

"We can't stay overnight. We have to go down south to work on the floats for the parade."

"On Christmas eve?" I knew they worked through the school vacation period, attaching millions of tiny seeds and flowers to the mechanized marvels that would prowl through Pasadena on New Year's Day and then be destroyed. A contemporary potlatch.

"Oh, no. Right after Christmas. We have to go to Jake's parents tomorrow night." She made a face.

No wonder she had forgotten that part of it. His parents disapproved of their son's unconventional lifestyle and marriage.

"I'm pregnant," she blurted out.

I sensed the conflict. She didn't say going to have a baby.

"I don't know what to do."

"How far along are you?" I stopped arranging the canapes to look at her, wearing rhinestone studded shirt and tight jeans tucked into cowboy boots. She didn't look pregnant.

"Oh, that isn't it." Jennifer seemed to realize my meaning. "I don't know whether to tell the Lindholms, Jake's family," she added at the blank look on my face. I had forgotten their family name since Jennifer had kept her maiden name, and we hardly ever saw Jake.

"It will make Christmas for Jake even worse to have them complaining that we have no business having a child when we can't even support ourselves."

"Then don't tell them."

Jennifer grinned. "And cancel Christmas?"

"Maybe you are needed in Pasadena, after all." It seemed a shame such a happy occasion couldn't be celebrated by his family. "Does Kathryn know?"

"Oh, yes. This is to be a little Kathryn, we've been informed, or we'll be cut out of the will."

"Or Phillip, if it's a boy," Kathryn entered the kitchen to come put her arms around Jennifer, her face wreathed in happy wrinkles.

Jasper Willard peered into the kitchen. "Can a fellow get a glass of water in here?" He nodded to Kathryn.

"Here. Let me get it." She turned to the cupboard to get a glass as though she were in her own kitchen.

Jennifer and I looked at each other with a flash of understanding.

Hot on his heels was Jeffrey Randall, festive in green sport coat and red tie.

"There you are, Kathryn. We need you for the soprano on *O Holy Night*." He managed to extricate her from the gathering in the kitchen, but Jasper dutifully followed them.

"Well, that's an interesting development." I was amazed.

"I don't think either of them even realize it yet," Jennifer observed.

"Is she feeling well?" I handed her plates to take out to the buffet.

"Phyllis says no extra excitement."

"Ha! Your aunt is an excitement junkie."

"She had to have Phyllis come out last week."

"I wondered if that was a house call or social, but didn't want to pry," I admitted.

"Ha! " Jennifer nudged my arm and I had to laugh even as I almost lost a plate of canapes onto the floor. My reputation preceded me. It was, after all, my profession to pry, which sometimes obscured the fact I was, by nature, downright nosy. But Jennifer had my number.

O Holy Night soared over the gathering, the faces of our neighbors and friends lifted in uncommon angelic fervor, with Armando's beautiful voice to inspire them. Guy and he had driven down that morning to stay over for Christmas, bringing armloads of presents to put under the little tree. I had a catch in my throat when thinking this might be Guy's last Christmas. Despite AZT his condition deteriorated, and his eyes took on a luminous glow as though every minute were becoming more and more precious.

Barbara came to help us put the fresh snacks on the dining room side table.

"I don't like having Randall here." She was tight-lipped.

"Neither do I. Maybe we can start a fight between him and Jasper."

"What?" Barbara looked at me like I was crazy.

I shrugged. "We'll think of something. Don't let his presence spoil our lovely party."

I returned to the kitchen to get a fresh pitcher of mulled cider. I liked to stay busy this way at social gatherings. It was the only time I missed the conviviality of an alcoholic beverage.

Making the rounds of the room, replenishing people's cups, was also an excellent way to speak to each guest and make sure they were comfortable. Just as I reached Jeffrey Randall, the singing had given way to debate about which carole to sing next.

"I hope you didn't mind my coming. Kathryn would have been disappointed if I had said no."

"Of course not. Would you like some more cider?" I took refuge in cold courtesy.

"I see you are a bird lover." He indicated the collection of bird ornaments on the Christmas tree.

"Bird watcher," I corrected him. "Or birder."

"These homes are lovely," he prattled on. "They don't build them like this anymore. A Craftsman, isn't it?"

He was looking at the massive fireplace, now home to a modern airtight woodstove, with the hallmark beveled glass cabinets on each side.

"Yes. Just like Kathryn's," I bit my lip to keep from saying more.

"Yours looks much bigger," he said.

"Only because we took out some walls." The hairs on the back of my neck prickled, and I could feel my jaw clench. I disliked discussing our house with him. Was he going to be after ours, too?

Hark the Herald Angels Sing drowned him out as I got away from him to attend to Phyllis, who stepped forward to have her cup filled.

"A lovely party, CC. Everyone is so jolly." The doctor seemed to be enjoying herself.

I nodded in recognition of our mutual plight. People weren't so happy when they came to see their doctor or their therapist. Else why would they go? It tended to skew our perspective of humankind as being generally depressed, cranky and miserable. We would forget that people could be cheerful and happy, too.

"Jeffrey has invited me to join the board." Phyllis ingested entire canapes lustily, washing them down with cider. "Such a nice thing for him to do. I've wanted to be more active in the community and this is a perfect opportunity."

I nodded and smiled, not trusting my voice. It was infuriating that he would be recruiting allies right in our own home.

Out of the corner of my eye, I caught an unlikely coupling. Guy and Vera were huddled in a corner in deep discussion. But, of course, if Vera could care about the homeless, she could also care about persons with HIV.

Blakely and Theresa showed up late, close to eleven o'clock, apologizing for having to be on duty.

"We have a checkpoint going and we're catching too many people."

"Consider the alternative." Theresa believed every drunk driver apprehended meant two lives saved.

Talk turned to the neighborhood sniper, with relief expressed that the incidents seemed to have dwindled.

I noticed Jasper seemed uncomfortable but I was too late to head him off from speaking.

"I think you all should know that I was one of the rifle shooters. I have since stopped doing it."

The gathering was hushed immediately.

"Why, Jasper?" Kathryn alone spoke.

"I'm not sure. I guess it had something to do with Abby's dying and my grieving. But it's all worked out now." Jasper faced his neighbors. "I'm real sorry to cause anyone worry."

"Someone is still doing it, then," Blakely said. "We're still getting reports."

"I must have set someone else off."

I watched Jeffrey but he was guarded, feigning disinterest, is what it looked like to me.

"Well, I appreciate your speaking up," Kathryn said. "It must have been difficult for you."

"Twenty-five years ago, no one would think a thing of it," a burly contractor said. "This was country and people had guns."

"What caliber of rifle did you use?" Jeffrey dared to ask. I dropped a coffeepot, creating some confusion about how to mop it up so it wouldn't stain the rug.

"Thank goodness, no one was burned," I said, but I didn't fool Barbara.

"Are you okay?" she asked me in the kitchen.

"I'd feel better if he were out of the house," I admitted.

Later in bed, we debated how much of an admission it was.

"He's rubbing our faces in it," I said indignantly.

"But hunters are always talking about what caliber of guns and types of shells. It may not have meant anything," Barbara disagreed.

"I know he's the other sniper. I know it in my bones."

"CC, you said yourself that there could be a lot of clients out there who have transferred resentments of their parents toward you. There could be someone else."

"That's not very reassuring." Somehow I expected my mate to be more agreeable to my point of view. I tended to forget she had her own mind and her own perspective.

"Better a client who is a loose cannon than Randall deliberately doing these things."

I had to admit she had a point. A client shooting my tire out was less frightening than Randall doing it. The client's behavior was somehow more normal in the context of things, and hopefully less dangerous. But it was hard to give up my obsession with Randall.

"Maybe he is using the rifle shooting to contribute to Kathryn's stress levels and raise her blood pressure."

"But it doesn't seem to be bothering her. It's you that it's hassling." Barb's voice was muffled into the pillow. I could take a hint that she wanted to go to sleep.

But I sat straight up in bed to look at her. It was a Eureka moment. "That's why Matt can't find any wrong doing in the San Diego board members' deaths. Randall found ways to hasten their natural demise."

"That is a big leap of fancy," Barb answered.

"I'll call Matt first thing in the morning. Perhaps it wasn't such a bad party after all." I snuggled into Barbara's back for warmth and promptly dropped off to sleep, exhausted but hopeful that some progress was being made.

Chapter 30

"What do you think of the idea that Randall may have contributed to their natural deaths?" I asked over the phone when Matt and I finally got together for a long distance discussion.

His end of the phone was silent. I realized it was a big jump from financial wrong doing.

"I don't see anything to support that, CC, although it's a fascinating theory." Matt was diplomatic. "Two of them were accidental deaths. One of those was a drunk driver. And the other three were natural dyings."

"What is your detective finding out?" I decided to drop the notion for now and try to be more open minded. By training and experience I might be too inclined to look for a pattern where there wasn't one.

"The drunk driver was a recovering alcoholic. Hadn't had a drink for fifteen years. Active in A.A. Then she relapsed and had an accident. Death was instantaneous."

"So much for anonymity," I observed.

"Oh, this detective is very good."

"Was there a precipitating incident?"

Matt was silent for a moment, obviously reading the report. "Depressed over death of sister."

"Could be plausible," I had to concede.

"Also, she was a librarian before she retired. Had known Randall for years."

"So you don't think Randall had anything to do with her death." I made a face at Barbara across the room in her reading chair.

"Doesn't look like it."

"Did she talk to her roommate, Emily Macias?"

"Yes. Nothing other than confirmation of the depression."

'Was your detective able to get the accident report?"

"Yes, I'll send it to you along with all the rest of the reports as they come in. She's still working on the three natural deaths. It's hard to get the medical profession to release such information."

"How about the other accidental death?" I noticed Barbara's renewed interest, even putting down the Katherine Forrest mystery she was reading.

"Fell and hit his head on the bathtub."

"Were there any witnesses?"

Matt's end of the phone line fell silent again as he looked for the information.

"A neighbor found him a day after the accident. He lived alone."

"Did he have any visitors?"

"The police didn't really investigate it. Ruled it an accidental death."

"Do you think the detective could find out more?"

"You still think it's foul play?" Matt's voice was skeptical again.

"Yes. There have been incidents here. I suspect that Jeffrey is very talented at making things look like accidents when they're not."

"We'll keep working on it. I'll send you what we have to date."

"Is he losing interest?" Barbara asked after I hung up.

"Not really. Discouraged, perhaps. But he's good for the long haul. He won't give up easily now." I needed to affirm this more for myself than about Matt.

Blakely was skeptical too, when I produced the preliminary findings several days later.

"There's still nothing really to go on, CC. No hard evidence. Not any factual data. We can't predicate an investigation on suspicion, no matter how well founded in psychological experience."

I had to smile at his diplomacy. "My therapy experience is probably more of a hindrance than a help."

"That doesn't mean I don't share your concern. I haven't ruled out the possibility of wrong doing." Blakely was careful, professional. He had even turned down coffee and carrot cake.

I hoped this meant he was starting to take this seriously, although it was more likely he was beginning to see my meddling as a problem and wanted to distance himself, separating the professional from the personal. I realized, too, what a pleasant friend Blakely had turned out to be, for a straight male. I didn't want to lose him.

"We think Randall was responsible for the school

board's dropping Barbara from the substitute rolls." I hoped to pique his interest again.

"Why would he do that?" Blakely was reserved.

"As a warning for us to back off investigating what went on in San Diego. The same reason for which he shot out my tire."

"This is red neck country." He dropped his guard. "I've been threatened myself. There was a sign in my locker at work. Most officers are fairly liberal but there are two homophobes."

"What did it say?" Randall's influence could have penetrated the sheriff's department as easily as the school board.

"Lezzie lover." Blakely looked uncomfortable.

"For being friends with us?" It was incredulous. "Randall must be networking with the good old boys."

"These two have harassed me before." He implied that Jeffrey couldn't have been responsible.

"He could have encouraged it. Incited them. Made fun of you. You know how men can do that."

I could not let go, at the risk of Blakely thinking I'm paranoid, obsessing on Jeffrey Randall like this, seeing him behind every incident, every accident. But I had the shell from his cottage for courage.

"The irony is that these two are very close drinking buddies. You would think they were gay themselves."

"They are the worst. It's the ones whose true feelings are the most denied and repressed who have to act them out."

"Yes, he doth protesteth too much. I know." Blakely was rueful.

Chapter 31

The next morning I ran some errands. First to the bank, a small one in the middle of town that provided plenty of parking, so I liked to go inside, leaving the drive-up window for folks who couldn't make the regular hours. The Central Coast Bank is a local home grown product that made good. Starting with one disgruntled major bank customer, they offered low interest loans to farmers, then eventually expanded to six branches throughout the area from Paso Robles to Santa Barbara. I could kick myself that I didn't buy stock when I had a chance. It's value has multiplied ten times.

Stationed at the door was a homeless person holding a Crisco can with a slit cut in the top for offerings. His clothes were stiff with greasy dirt, his hair straggly, a graying beard drooping down his chest. He reeked of ketones.

I was struck with a pang that it was alcoholics and

the mentally ill who were most affected by our administration's heartless policies towards the homeless.

As though reading me like a book, he said, "Can you help out the homeless, lady?"

I looked into his eyes, no different than my own. Twinkling and deep blue. Amused at my interest no doubt.

I handed over a five and started to move on, then stopped. "Do you know about Shelterworks here in town?"

"Yes. I thought I'd go there tonight." His speech was precise, educated. This was no derelict. This was a mighty who had fallen.

Disturbed by the encounter, I took a drive by Shelterworks although I didn't have any evaluations or reports to offer. Randall's Mercedes was not in evidence.

I'll use concern about Kathryn's blood pressure, I decided, as an excuse for stopping by.

Vera was pleasant, inviting me into her office and offering a cup of tea. I had come at a good time as it was a half hour before client hours.

Today, I could focus more on the agency itself.

"This is quite a nice operation." I had to admire the decorating job of blues and greens and white pine office furniture.

"Yes, just because we serve the disenfranchised, doesn't mean we have to look like a soup kitchen." Vera beamed with pride as she bustled about fixing our tea.

"How do you do it?" I leaped to my chance.

"Mr. Randall is able to get funds from all sorts of sources. Merchants donated most of the furnishings."

"And the building?" I noticed it was a fairly new wing of a county services complex.

"The board of supervisors is happy to furnish us space, particularly because we are providing services for no additional county money." Vera sounded like she was reading out of their brochure.

"Someone is paying your salaries and the utilities," I persisted.

"State and federal funds are available for those needs. Also, as a nonprofit entity, Shelterworks has already received some sizable donations from corporate and private citizens."

"May I ask who they are?"

Vera hesitated, looking at me suspiciously. "Why do you want to know?"

I took a deep breath and plunged right in. "I have reason to believe Jeffrey may be engaged in some questionable practices."

"Like what?"

"I can't say precisely, but there have been incidences both here and in San Diego that suggest wrong doing."

Vera gazed at me for a long time as though studying my innermost depths. I had seen that look before on client's faces, as they tried to decide whether or not to trust me with their secrets.

Finally, she spoke. "We do seem to be fiscally well endowed, more than one would expect. I believe Mr. Randall is from a wealthy family. He used his own funds as collateral for bank loans and matching subsides from the federal government. However, he plans that Shelterworks will be completely self-sufficient by next fiscal year."

"How does he plan to do that? What about the

housebuilding aspect of the operation?" I persisted.

"I think I would be way out of line to disclose anymore to you, CC. You might discuss this with Kathryn Montecito."

"It's because of Kathryn that I need to know."

"How is that?" Vera's attention returned.

"She has high blood pressure. Her doctor says no excitement. I'm afraid the officer elections might be too taxing."

"Oh, it's all arranged beforehand. It's not like a political election."

"But what about the responsibility?"

"She's just a symbolic community representative. We do all the work." Vera smiled reassuringly.

"What do you mean?" This wasn't going exactly the way I had hoped, but like a therapy session, people could take you on surprising twists and turns and bring you to a destination wholly unanticipated.

"All Kathryn has to do is chair the meetings. The agenda is prepared before hand. Anyone could do it."

"What about debate? And parliamentary procedure?"

"That's the purpose of Robert's Rules of Order. To allow civilized discussion of the issues and come to a consensus decision."

I had to grin. "Who was Robert, anyway? I always meant to find out."

Vera smiled back. "Henry M. Robert was an engineering officer in the Army in the late 1800's. A very interesting man. He wanted to free public meetings from confusion and dispute."

"Trust an engineer to want order," I said.

Vera looked away, then seemed to have come to a decision.

"There is something I would like to show you. In confidence," she warned.

"Absolutely."

Vera arose from her desk and left the room for a few minutes, returning with a file of newspaper clippings.

They were obits of local citizens. Yellow felt tip shaded the names of survivors, widows and widowers both.

"It's one thing to be nice to your benefactors. It's quite another to go out and recruit grieving elders."

"A bit blood thirsty," I agreed.

"Opportunistic, to say the least. I must confess I feel uneasy with it, although there is no real wrong doing."

"But there may very well be real wrong doing."

"How is that?" Vera gathered up the clippings and put them back in the file.

"Randall may be contributing to people's natural deaths. That's why I'm concerned about Kathryn."

"I don't see how. He doesn't even know these people."

"But he obviously plans to come to know the survivors."

"To recruit them as members of the foundation." Vera seemed a bit testy, but I couldn't stop now.

"And persuade them to provide for Shelterworks in their wills."

"Yes. That's not out of line for nonprofit organizations. United Way, hospitals, The Salvation Army. They all do it." She looked at me as though even a person as obsessed as I could see the reasonableness of this.

"But what about them deeding their property over

to Shelterworks while they're still alive?"

"That's acceptable, too. Works out nicely for elderly people. They can use their money to travel and enjoy life instead of having limited incomes eaten up by taxes and maintenance expenses. Sure beats these reverse mortgages."

"Unless their life span is uh, foreshortened, before they get a chance to have all that fun."

"Is that what you suspect?" Vera shook her head.

"I know it's unthinkable, when your agency is doing so much good for so many." Damnation! I'd gone too far with her.

She rose, looking at her watch. "I'm afraid I have to see people now."

"I really appreciate your showing me those. Could I by chance have copies?"

"No. I'm afraid I can't do that. Loyalty to," she hesitated, "the agency."

I let it go. If worse came to worse, Vera was too honest not to testify as to what she knew and saw. Now that the seeds of suspicion were planted, she might even come forward of her own volition, especially if there is any future dubious activity by Jeffrey.

"Would you mind not telling Randall I was here?"

"Not unless he asks."

I was satisfied at having found yet another piece of the puzzle. Soon there would be enough to make a case against Randall and stop him from harming other helpless elders.

There was the problem of Blakely, however. The more evidence I produced, the more he seemed to balk. His loyalty would always be to other men, not a woman, and certainly not a lesbian. It was a reality I had to face and accept. But it was lonely to feel one's friend slip away. And I saw a chasm of depression yawning beneath the alienation—classic separation anxiety.

Chapter 32

"She looks more like an aerobics instructor than an attorney."

Barb sounded disapproving. We were watching out the window as Dolly Han leaped out of her luxury import car and bounded up the walk to our front door.

Electric blue lycra tights, a green sweatshirt, permed wild hair and makeup, she seemed like a kid right off the pages of *Sassy*, but I knew she had to be at least forty-five.

"Doesn't look like a sister, either," I had to say.

"Lipstick lesbian," Barbara murmured just before she threw open the door to greet her.

"Since I was going to be in Pismo this weekend, it seemed a good idea to bring by your court petitions for signatures." The morning January sunshine flared behind her like a halo around our own angel.

"What exactly are the documents for?" Barb asked

as soon as we had arranged ourselves on the chintz sofas.

"To file suit in the civil court for wrongful termination of employment and emotional distress."

"That's for sure," I approved.

"Illegal discrimination is the basis of the suit," Dolly continued as she rummaged around in a battered canvas briefcase. "I recommend we ask for a trial without a jury."

"Why no jury?" Barbara asked.

"In civil cases only six jurors serve. That doesn't give you very good odds for overcoming most people's prejudice."

"That's not very encouraging. You mean we stand a better chance with a judge?" I was disappointed.

"Yes, he or she will be more liberal, less affected by their own homophobia. By training they can stick to the issues."

"Not in this county," Barbara argued. "The school board has a lot of political power and can influence both the board of supervisors and the judges."

"All the more reason that I'm recommending a change of venue to Santa Barbara. That won't be too difficult a commute for either of us."

"Good idea." My hopefulness returned.

"Don't be invested in the outcome," cautioned the attorney. "Let's just give it our very best shot."

"How about some coffee or tea?" I remembered to be hospitable.

"Just water, please." Dolly smiled in vibrant healthfulness.

It was disgusting. I filled one of our jazzy parrot glasses with water and arranged fruit slices—some apple, pear and oranges—on a Portugal flower plate.

I knew a more healthful diet and exercise could reduce my short windedness. It was hard to accept aging. I wanted my body to do what it used to do—walking fast uphill, leaping from rock to rock at the river, taking steps two at a time. Middle-age was difficult because youth was not that far behind. Inside I was still twelve, whizzing down the streets on a bicycle; running furiously to make a field goal as though my very life depended on it; climbing the hills above our neighborhood in the Ventura avenues to look down from a godlike place. I wanted it all back.

As I brought the tray to the living room, I came back to the present. I was just envious of Dolly, of her youthful exuberance. Our cozy home and serene lifestyle was what I most cherished. I poured the tea for me and Barbara. After all, one couldn't deny oneself every pleasant thing. Some poet said there were fewer agreeable moments in life than those taking tea. We had a good life, despite the current obstacles. Even if Barbara didn't get her job back, we would be all right without it. And if worse came to worse, we could always move north where, despite AIDS backlash, there was still less homophobia.

The contentment was all too short lived. After signing the petitions, we showed Dolly around our homestead. As we stepped out onto the back terrace, nothing prepared us for the carnage that assaulted our eyes.

Dead birds were everywhere. Finches, sparrows, mourning doves and titmice were strewn about like little soldiers on a miniature battleground.

I rushed around to each tiny body, a few of which were still struggling, but even those fell quiet as we watched them die, helplessly.

Dolly was the first to speak. “My god. I’ve never seen anything like this. Life in the country is brutal. There must be a hundred dead birds out here.”

“Not this brutal. This isn’t natural.” My voice choked and I set to rushing about, picking up the birds and examining them, performing a kind of triage to see if any survivors could benefit from a veterinarian’s attention.

Barbara went to the bird feeder some fifty feet out into the middle of the pasture—The Restaurant we called it because it was so big and served so many.

“I think the birdseed was poisoned.” She sniffed the unfamiliar seed.

I gave up trying to save any of the birds. Despair was making my eyes wild. A hot rage came over me, but I forced it down, to pay attention to the kernels in Barbara’s hand.

“Yes, you’re right. That’s not the seed we use. Could be strychnine or Compound 1080. Ranchers used it to kill squirrels before environmental concern caused feed store owners to stop carrying it.” I remembered discussions about predators and chemical toxins.

“No wonder it didn’t take much to kill them if it’s formulated for squirrels.” Dolly just kept shaking her head.

“Do you suppose someone made a mistake?” Barbara was obviously reluctant to ascribe human intention to such cruelty.

“Randall did this. I’ll get him for this.” I knew for the first time in my life I was capable of hurting, killing even, or maiming another human being. Breaking through to the rage deep within was an uncivilized alternative to the cold bank of depression.

In a slicing arc of insight I realized my father had been depressed to keep from falling into this maelstrom. I had always known it in my mind, but now every fiber of my body knew this truth about my father, about myself.

"No, no!" Dolly was firm. "We'll get him through the court. We'll add this to our complaint. This will cost him plenty of money. There is the expense of cleaning up. Harmful effects on the environment. We might even get some extra environmental protection penalties. I'll research it first thing Monday morning."

I heard her words but all I could register was the grisly carnage strewn all over our land.

Barbara went in the house to return with a camera.

"Better document it for evidence."

"We'll have to prove it. Make some connection to Randall with this seed." I once again was stymied by the lack of a direct link to my nemesis.

Barbara and Dolly exchanged looks.

"Oh, no you don't. Don't be getting any ideas about playing detective." Barbara was adamant. "Turn it over to Blakely and Theresa and let them investigate."

"Absolutely. Everytime you do something like that, there seems to be a reciprocal event." Dolly watched me, waiting for her meaning to sink in.

"Are you saying I am causing these things to happen?" I threw the bird seed down in a tantrum, very unlike myself.

"I'm not saying it's your fault, CC. It's just that there does seem to be a sequence of escalating events." Dolly's voice was kind. I recognized her finesse as my own in leading a client to just such an awareness of their behavior.

"But if I do nothing, he gets away with..." I didn't finish it. My god, was it possible that I was unwittingly helping to make it happen? That Kathryn could be murdered because of my meddling. That if I left it alone, none of these events would be taking place? I faced fully the arrogance of my own willfulness as I saw the drastic consequences of my actions, no matter how honorably motivated.

Blakely sniffed at the bird seed and looked over the death scene.

"I've heard of a bacteria getting in the bird feeders that can be deadly. From the birds themselves."

"Yes, if you don't keep the feeders clean. We clean these out regularly with a bleach solution." I was patient and humble, still chastened by my realization I may have contributed to this carnage around us.

"Lots of ranchers have poisoned feed for squirrel control," Blakely said.

"I know. But it doesn't wind up in our bird feeder." I maintained my patience.

"Yes, but someone could have made a mistake at the feedstore. Put the wrong seed in your order."

"Blakely, look at this sample of seed. Now look at mine. The two piles formed little cones sitting on paper towels.

"I'm sorry, CC. They look the same to me."

"This one has more nut meats and sunflower seeds." I pointed to the sample from the bird feeder. "It's higher priced stuff. We mix our own with more millet." I indicated the plain round seeds songbirds favored. "To make it stretch further. When you go through fifty pounds a month, you need some economy."

"But I just can't tell a judge I want a warrant to go searching some pillar of the community's home for poisoned seed. Don't you see?"

"Well then, who can?" I was losing patience. "I'll bet you could if it were the other way around. If Randall accused us of something. You're just like all straight men, not taking us seriously."

"It's not that." Blakely seemed contrite. "The sheriff had a little talk with me."

"Oh, the good old boys. Great." I didn't like this at all.

"He thinks my professional judgment is biased in favor of gays. He has warned me to be more impartial or I'm out."

"Oh, Blakely." I held back from heaping scorn on him for putting his job considerations ahead of friendship. I had no right to ask that of him. We mere mortals operate on enlightened self interest. Better to have him in the department than no friend at all.

"What about Theresa?" At least she wouldn't be caught up in the good old boys' dynamic.

"I'll talk to her. See if she wants to investigate it. She sees this sort of thing as small potatoes compared to the child abuse and wife battering cases that she takes."

"This is gay abuse, Blakely."

He tried to explain. "I'm caught in the middle. There is no case, yet. I'll lose my job if I investigate Randall at this stage."

"Meaning if someone gets hurt or killed, then you'll investigate."

"Right."

He was serious, I realized.

"I'm going to clean this mess up. It's starting to smell and I don't want the vultures to take it into the food chain." I took a large plastic garbage bag from the garden tool shed and began bagging the birds.

"We have pictures of all this, if Theresa is interested in investigating further."

"Don't get your hopes up, CC. Not in this county." Blakely shook his head.

No doubt he had protected me from the full force of his colleagues' prejudice, I flushed at this unspoken warning. I tended to forget there was more tolerance for lesbians and gays in my therapy world. Most of straight, especially rural America, was still prejudiced. Especially against teachers or women who make waves, or didn't accept the edicts of the straight male system. It's enough to make me want a revolution.

Liberals, radical women and gays coming together to construct a new government based on concensus process. Hierarchical organizations would be swept out with egalitarian employee owned companies striving for excellence, reaping the profits of their own efforts. Perhaps no multi-millionnaires or billionnaires, but there wouldn't need to be any homeless or disenfranchised either.

"I'll have Theresa get in touch with you." Blakely broke through my fantasy.

I knew he was suffering, too, conflicted between keeping his job and loyalty to a friend. It was obvious which had prevailed and hard not to blame him. I had to remember it wasn't his fault. Depression sagged beneath me like treacherous quicksand.

Chapter 33

I was still feeling depressed over the poisoning of the birds when I took the last part of my program report to Vera. Although it was almost ten o'clock and clients were already forming a line, the office was closed. A note pinned to the door read: *Be back soon. Thank you for waiting.*

Jeffrey Randall pulled into the parking lot and came to the office door.

"What's this? What's going on?" He looked at me like I should know something.

"I have no idea. I just arrived myself."

He unlocked the office, ignoring the clients. I slipped in behind him, thinking to leave my report on Vera's desk.

"She has no business doing this." I heard him mutter.

I watched through the open door to his office as he read a note.

"Is there anything I can do to help?" I couldn't resist pitching in on an emergency even if it was for him.

"There's been an accident at the building site. She's gone to attend to it."

"Would you like me to stay here and take care of the clients?" I wasn't unmindful of the opportunity to get a look at his files.

"No, thank you. Vera should have stayed here." He wadded her note up and threw it in the wastepaper can. He looked like he would like to kick it.

"I'll just put this report on Vera's desk." I moved toward her office.

"Let me have it." He stepped into my path.

I handed it over, finding his reaction to this business quite strange. He seemed more concerned about Vera's protocol than the fact that someone may have been injured.

"I have to go now. I'm going to lock the office back up." He went to the front door and indicated I should leave, too. Dutifully I followed.

Outside, the line of clients surged forward and then halted. There was a protesting groan. Randall dashed to his car and sped away. Naturally, I followed him to the construction site.

An ambulance was backed up to the first house, a completed model.

Medics were attending to someone. It was Normand, the electrician. Vera was holding his hand.

"What happened, for God's sake?" Jeffrey's voice crackled.

"Normand's had a bad jolt. Something was wrong with the wiring." Vera answered him but continued to attend to her friend. "I'm going to the hospital with him until Petey, that's his wife, can get there."

"What time will that be?" Jeffrey sounded peeved. "You have appointments to keep."

"When I can get there."

The ambulance screamed away. Jeffrey turned to the bystanders. "Does anyone know what happened?"

A small wiry man wearing a carpenter's apron came forward. "Someone didn't follow Normand's instructions on the wiring. When he went to throw the juice on and check to see everything was right, he got a hell of a shock."

"Who did that?" Jeffrey demanded to know.

No one answered.

He tried a different approach. "Whose house is this?"

"That don't matter," said one of the women in coveralls and boots. "We all work on all the houses."

"It won't help to cover up this matter. It will be investigated, I can assure you of that."

The group was sullen and quiet, waiting to see what he would do next. Jeffrey whirled on his heel and left the scene. It was apparent to me that Randall may be a bigtime administrator, fiscally, but his people skills were worse than nil. He actually inspired negative reactions. I could see it all over their faces. Somehow, it was a small vindication of my continued suspicions of him.

Ever the psychologist, I pondered his disclosures in the cabin that day—how feeling himself to blame for his father's death could make him so focused on control and order that he could deny himself any humanitarian concern for fellow flesh and blood human beings. The emotional abuse by his alcoholic father had contributed to a rigid need for order to compensate for a childhood of chaos and confusion. Thus today he was obsessed with protocol and rules to avoid unexpected events. I worried that an accident like this would be enough to precipitate a psychotic break.

"Was he hurt badly?" I turned to the woman in coveralls.

"He's not dead, but he got burned real bad." She seemed to relax with me. "What do you think we should do?"

"Maybe close down for the day. Give people a chance to get over the shock," I counseled.

"That's a good idea." The first man in the carpenter's apron took charge. "Let's take up a collection for flowers."

The building program looked fascinating but this didn't feel like the right time to look it over. I decided to go to the hospital.

Vera was pacing the hall.

"Oh, CC, it looks real bad. He's in intensive care."

"I'm sorry, Vera." There was nothing else to do but put my arms around her and try to comfort her.

"Petey's with him now."

I sat with her quietly until Petey came out an hour or so later.

"He's going to make it." Tears were in her eyes as she embraced her friend.

"Thank you for coming, CC." She held out her hand which I took and held, warming it in my own.

"Thank God." Vera began to cry in relief.

"He has extensive burns. It will be a long siege of skin grafts and surgeries." Petey's voice was clear and strong and determined.

I winced. There was nothing more prolonged and tortured than a burn victim's plight. My mind flashed on napalm victims at the Veteran's hospital. The awful thing is that painkillers don't work because the skin isn't there to hold the chemicals in.

Vera recovered herself and announced, "I have to go back to the office. Shall I come over after work?"

"Yes, please. I need you to be with me," Petey hugged her friend again.

"Would you like me to take you?" Somehow I knew Randall hadn't attended to those clients and Vera was going to have her hands full.

"Yes, I'd appreciate that, unless Petey..." She hesitated.

"No. I'm going to stay here awhile. Thanks anyway."

Vera broke our silence on the drive back. "It was a stupid mistake."

"Most accidents are. But we are imperfect beings. We make mistakes." Somewhere it got writ that we were supposed to be perfect. It was hard to teach people that errors were an integral part of the human experience.

At the office, we pitched in together to take care of the clients. Most needed emergency room and meal vouchers—hots and a cot—which we were able to dispense immediately and cut the crowd down to a few candidates for the building program.

Randall emerged from his office then.

"Normand is in intensive care but he's going to make it," Vera told him.

"Did he say what happened?" Jeffrey frowned.

"I doubt that he even knew. What did you find out when you were at the site?" Vera reversed the interrogation.

He glanced at me as though looking for corroboration. "I tried to investigate. They closed ranks on me. Just like enlisted men."

"Normand has extensive burns. He'll need many skin grafts."

"You better check the insurance coverage." He sighed. "I think there are some limitations on the number of surgeries allowed."

"I closed the site down for the rest of the week. An investigator from the county needs to check out everything for a detailed report."

Vera gave him a message slip.

"I thought the clients needed a break, anyway. The accident scared them."

"Humph. As well it should. Teach them to be more careful. Follow instructions."

"The investigator asked for us to be available. She'll have to interview us both."

"Just what we need. More snooping around." He glared at me. "More problems and more delays. And with this county bureaucracy, it will be weeks before we're back on schedule."

"I'm just grateful he wasn't killed." Vera looked at me pointedly. I could tell she was getting angry.

"Friend of yours, was he?"

"A very dear friend. He and his wife have been very good to me over the years. I owe them a lot."

"I hope this situation isn't going to interfere with your functioning here. Things are going to be difficult enough with the investigation."

Vera and I looked at each other in disbelief. We were so unimportant in the scheme of things that he didn't even bother to hide his insensitivity. I suspected he was so focused on the problems caused by the accident, he'd become blinded to the larger picture. He probably wasn't even aware of it. It made me all the more certain he was capable of murder.

Chapter 34

"Five people are dead. Kathryn's next and we can't seem to do a damn thing about it!" I pumped frustration out on my rowing machine.

"Have you forgotten the Serenity Prayer?" Barbara admonished.

"Lord, grant me the serenity to accept the things I cannot change, the courage to change the things I can and the wisdom to know the difference." Dutifully I recited the AA mantra. Although seeming to be merely a variant of the old-fashioned count to ten, it went deeper, acknowledging the many things mere mortals could do nothing about but accept. And in so doing, kept many an alcoholic from relapsing, including me.

But this was anger that could not be accepted, nor let go. I kept discharging as I worked out. "I know Randall's responsible, but we can't prove it. Blakely is useless. Our entire system of law and order is not working for us. It works for Randall, but forget it for women or gays, or the elderly. He's getting away with murder."

Barb had begun her warmups. "Maybe you're misjudging him, attributing acts to him that aren't so."

I stopped rowing to catch my breath. "I know he's up to something. I have a 30-06 shell from his cottage to prove it."

"I thought you must have something you weren't admitting." Barbara kept doing her arm swings, but glowered at me.

"The other thing is that every time I probe somewhere he pushes back."

Barbara looked at me worriedly.

"I admit I'm helping to make some things happen, like your job and the bird poisoning. But to stop the pressure for fear of retaliation is like giving in to terrorists. And I had nothing to do with what went on in San Diego." I reminded her.

"We have no proof that anything happened in San Diego. Matt just told you he can't get anything on the other three deaths."

"But that's all the more suspicious. Why not? Why such a complete blackout on three different dyings?" I hadn't accepted this last report very well at all.

"We really have nothing to go on. Except your shell. That is something at least. Maybe Blakely could do a ballistics test on Randall's rifle."

"No. He won't do anything unless someone gets killed." I was feeling pretty discouraged and then I remembered a possible lead.

"We have Emily Macias." My gloom lifted. I had asked Matt to have the investigator trace her whereabouts. She now lived in Santa Barbara, just two hours down the coast. The librarian had retired and moved north six months after her roommate's death.

Chapter 35

I knocked on the door of the small rose-guarded house on an elevated street near the Botanical Gardens. The drive south had been swift and purposeful. Emily Macias was my only hope of finding real evidence of wrongful death.

The compact woman who opened the door was wiry with close cropped iron-gray hair and liquid brown eyes with fire in their centers.

"Yes?" Her greeting was economical.

Beethoven's Sixth, the Pastorale, escaped outdoors into the January sunshine where it belonged.

I explained who I was and why I had come. Emily let me in, reluctantly.

"It's been two years since she died, Ms. Scott. I don't see how I can be of any help." Emily turned down the volume on the music and offered me coffee or tea.

"Coffee please, if it's already made."

"No problem to make it." She went to the kitchen, an alcove of the main room. It was an open house plan, with the dining area set off from the living room solely by its placement near the kitchen area.

Her movements were deft, with quick poise.

So this is what seventy looks like. There was a definite difference between a lesbian seventy and a straight seventy. Emily was still vigorous and quick moving, like a sparrow with a sense of flight even when on the ground. *Con Brio.*

We settled in at the dining room table with the coffee. Emily stared at me appraisingly. I felt a sensual stirring. By damn. She was still a very attractive lady.

"How did you find me?"

"A private investigator."

"Why do you think Charlotte's death may not have been an accident?" Emily was clearly in charge of this interrogation.

"I think I should tell you first of all that I am a recovered alcoholic myself."

She nodded.

"After sixteen years of sobriety, it would take an awful lot to make me relapse."

"What do you mean?"

"I wonder if she really relapsed."

"Her blood alcohol was .04. Not very much, but too much for an alcoholic. Enough to..." Emily's voice quavered.

"Yes, such a small amount. Alcoholics don't fool around with such meager amounts. If I were to relapse, you can bet I'd be in the .20 range. Blotto." I know without a doubt that I would never drink again, even as I fantasized the possibility for Emily's sake. I know I'd already drank up my share.

"I see what you mean." Emily was quiet.

"Where did she go the night of the accident?" I probed as gently as I could. This was sensitive territory.

"A bar."

"Ah, a slippery place." I acknowledged, using an old AA expression.

"She'd done it before. At her age. It was ridiculous. We were librarians, well known in the community. And all those younger women. She would drink cokes, but I knew sooner or later she'd slip up."

"It must have made you angry," I said.

"Yes, but you see, it was my fault."

Typical co-dependent, I noted, assuming the blame for the loved one's behavior.

"How was it your fault?"

"I was having an affair." Emily looked away in shame. "She was just trying to get even with me, trying to get me to pay attention to her again. Renew our relationship."

"I see. Can you tell me exactly what happened that night."

"She had a dinner to attend. I told her I would be late and not to wait up for me. She begged me not to go. Said she'd stay home too. If only I had." Emily's voice was full of remorse.

"Where was this dinner?" I hated to stir it all up again for her, but I knew she had some healing to do yet.

"At CARE. Charlotte was on the board of directors, as you must know."

"Do they serve alcohol?"

"A little wine. But she never drank it. Everyone knew she was a recovered alcoholic and went to some trouble to arrange substitute drinks for her."

"Like what?"

"Mulled ciders. Punch. Non-alcoholic wines."

"Did Jeffrey Randall attend to that?"

Emily nodded, looking at me with that molten fire. "Or his secretary."

"Either of them could have spiked her dinner drinks."

"That would account for the low blood level." Emily was following my train of thought.

"Maybe it wasn't your fault, at all." The therapist couldn't pass up an opportunity to relieve pain.

"You know, I never did like that man. And I didn't like Charlotte giving them so much, but it made her happy."

"What did she give them?" I could see from the house and furnishings that Emily was comfortable financially.

"Not our place. I'd never have stood for that." Her fire flashed. "But she gave them her sister's property. It was one of those estate planning situations where they made the payments, and then took the property when she..." Emily stopped short.

"How did her sister die?" I might be stretching it here, but neither did I want to leave loose ends.

"Kidneys. She was eighty years old. It was her time to go."

"So what happened the night of the accident?" I brought her back around.

"She left the bar, a women's bar of course, around eleven o'clock. They said she didn't drink. Just a coke. But I didn't believe them. They were just covering up for her." Emily got up from the table, agitated, and paced the room.

"We lived near Balboa Park. She was almost home

when she lost control and ran into the center divider. It was concrete. A head-on collision. Her head smashed into the windshield."

I winced at the imagery thinking how often she must have conjured it up over and over, punishing herself. I pushed the picture of it being Barbara out of my mind.

"No apparent reason for losing control?"

"They checked the scene of the accident. There was a bottle in the car. The cause of accident was chalked up to the alcohol."

"No forensics done on the car?"

"Not that I know of. The car went straight to the salvage yard."

"What was the bottle?"

"Bourbon. Jack Daniels."

"Was that her drink when she was practicing?"

"No. She drank scotch. But no one thought anything of that at the time."

"If I'm going to relapse after years of abstinence, I'm going to have my favorite stuff."

"What are you saying?" Emily frowned, sitting back down at the table.

"I am thinking that Jeffrey Randall could have spiked her punch and planted the bottle in her car."

"But what about the accident?"

"Without a forensics report, how do we know something else caused her to lose control?" I knew .04 wasn't enough to impair someone's driving that much, although I'm the first to advocate for no drinking and driving at all.

"I think Randall caused me to almost have an accident by shooting out my tire on a bridge."

Emily nodded, her liquid brown eyes wide as she

pictured the scene again. "The window was shattered. But that was from her head. The highway patrol must have examined everything well enough to find a bullet."

"Maybe it wasn't a bullet. Maybe it was the brakes, or a light shining in her eyes." I was starting to think like my nemesis. I could imagine all sorts of ways to do away with people. He must be my shadow. My disowned self.

Emily shook her head. "I never thought for a moment it could have happened otherwise, but now I don't know. Maybe she didn't relapse. Maybe it wasn't my fault. But none of this is going to bring Charlotte back." Tears shone in her pretty brown eyes.

"How long were you together?" My voice was like a lover's.

"Thirty-four years. We worked together, lived together, traveled to Europe, Australia. It was a good life. The affair was my fault. I succumbed to another woman's charms. It didn't mean anything, though. Just my ego needing some attention."

I nodded. How many times I had heard that lament. What people didn't seem to realize is that they didn't have to act on those attractions. Just experience them, enjoy them and let them pass. And hardly ever was an affair solely one partner's fault.

"She probably knew that," I said.

"I thought she did, until the accident..." Her voice trailed off.

"What happened to the car, by the way." I remembered to go back to it.

"I sold it to a wrecking yard. I was executor of her estate. Might still be there. They salvage the parts."

My hopes leaped up. This could be it. This could be the break I was looking for.

"What are you going to do?" Emily's voice was sharp.

"Check out the car. See if San Diego might reopen the case."

Emily looked uncomfortable. "It won't bring her back."

"No, but it might help keep someone else from being killed, accidently."

"I'm trying to put together a new life."

I nodded.

"I don't want any publicity. I have family here."

"We'll be discreet," I promised. I knew family was very important to the old lineages of Spanish nobility that once owned most of the state. That pride did not allow for alternative life styles.

But if this case broke open the way I thought it might, I knew Emily would forgive the news coverage.

Chapter 36

"I'm sorry, CC. The car is long gone. Its parts were sold off and the shell flattened for scrap metal."

"Another damned dead end." I was furious. "Fate is conspiring against us. It's not fair."

"There is no justice," Matt softly answered.

I was caught up short. How many times I had to remind clients of this very same thing. It was irrational to expect life to be fair. Life was not fair. Sometimes things went your way, sometimes not.

"But Emily has told you enough to cast suspicion on the circumstances of Charlotte's death." He granted me a reprieve.

"True. What about the colonel's accident? Has your investigator talked to his neighbor?"

"Yes. The neighbor knew him well. Intimately, I might add. She claims he was fit as a fiddle and not at all clumsy."

"Not a likely candidate for slipping in the bathtub."

"No. But I don't see how we can prove it."

At least Matt wasn't telling me to give it up. But maybe it was time for me to face reality. Perhaps I was in the grips of an obsession.

"I wonder how much crime people get away with for lack of evidence?" I felt myself dropping into despair. My father's depression lurked in waiting.

Chapter 37

I was in the chicken coop, putting fresh wood shavings in the nests of our big Rhode Island Reds, when a scream of brakes was followed by a thudding crash. It sounded nearby, just up the road. I ran out of the barn and through the orchard to the roadway in clumsy rubber boots.

The Call-a-ride van and a blue car had collided. Seniors staggered out of the van. I immediately dashed into the house and dialed 911, knowing a few minutes could make a significant difference.

Then I grabbed a handful of clean dishtowels and

ran up the road, huffing and puffing, to see if anyone needed first aid. The van squat at an angle to the blue car, with the fenders of both vehicles crumpled into each other. The Call-a-ride driver was attending to passengers who seemed the most shaken.

"I didn't see the car. The sun was in my eyes. It was my fault." The van driver took responsibility. A distinguished looking gentleman, he looked like he could be retired himself.

"It doesn't look like anyone is hurt too bad." He noticed my armful of towels.

"I had the right of way. He ran right into me." The other driver sported a trickle of blood on her forehead.

"Are you all right?" She seemed to be the only one visibly injured.

"Yes. Just a scratch." She dabbed at her head with a tissue.

"I called 911." I turned back to the driver of the van.

"Thank you." He continued to attend to his charges worriedly. "Are you okay, Cody? Mrs. Anderson?" He called his passengers by name.

A woman in a sweatsuit stepped out of the van, limping slightly. "Guess I won't be running a marathon, today."

Everyone laughed at the well-timed levity. In the distance we could hear an ambulance siren.

Of the five passengers, three men and two women, none seemed to require immediate attention, although I would certainly feel better when everyone's vital signs had been checked by the medics.

The driver of the car continued to fret. "I'm going to be late for an appointment. Could I use your telephone?"

"I believe you aren't to leave the scene of an accident until the authorities arrive. Would you like me to call for you?" I offered to do this even though this woman's attitude irritated me. She had shown no concern for the elderly passengers in the van and was so quick to blame the other driver. And instead of counting her blessings the accident hadn't been worse, the woman was focused on minor inconvenience. My annoyance with this woman was a therapeutic signal. Perhaps another shadow self I did not like.

"Your neighbor just missed all the fun." A gentleman in a warm-up suit spoke up.

"Oh, how is that?" I went on alert. He meant Kathryn.

"Kathryn was supposed to go to the library with us, but she wasn't ready. Said she'd go later this morning."

I knew this wasn't an accident. It was Randall again. Somehow he caused this to happen.

Theresa pulled up in a black and white just seconds ahead of the ambulance.

"What happened, CC?" Theresa asked, leading me a bit away from the scene of the accident so the others didn't hear us.

"The driver of the van was blinded by a light. He didn't see the blue car and turned left into her path." I pointed out the original positions of the two vehicles.

"Theresa, I think it was Randall again."

The sheriff's deputy looked at me like she thought I was crazy, shaking her head. Then she went to the driver of the van to take his statement.

Humiliated, I slunk back home to the chicken coop to finish my chores, mulling over the scene. The sun had not been in the right position to blind the van driver. Why hadn't Theresa been willing to see that? Perhaps the bias of the young about the faculties of the middle-aged.

Later that afternoon, I worked up my courage to go over to see Kathryn.

"That was a close call this morning," I observed.

"Yes. Thank goodness no one was really hurt. Just Millie and she's having a ball getting all that attention." Kathryn turned off the sound of Oprah in deference to my company, but continued to sneak glances at the picture.

I had to smile. The senior grapevine worked with dispatch.

"I have to ask you something that might sound strange."

"Yes?" Kathryn leaned forward.

"Did Randall know of your intention to take the Call-a-ride to the library this morning?"

Kathryn's eyes narrowed. "What are you getting at? You think Jeffrey had something to do with the accident?"

"I don't know. Indulge me, Kathryn. Did he?"

"No. No reason for him to know that. I don't keep him informed of my daily activities."

"Could he have found out from Call-a-ride?"

"I suppose."

It was natural that Kathryn should resist this possibility. After all, it was unthinkable that someone so attentive could intend her harm. It was something the mind would not easily wrap itself around.

"You know, CC, sometimes accidents are really just accidents."

I felt the peculiar ache of loneliness that comes from no one believing in you. I was again marching to a drummer no one else even admitted existed much less heard. A deviant always. Different. Misunderstood.

You're having a separation anxiety attack, I counseled myself. No small thing. I was glad Barbara wasn't home to witness my setback, having gone into San Luis on an errand regarding her case against the school board.

Action. Taking action was what was needed. All these incidents are not accidents. There was a pattern and it would trace back to Jeffrey Randall.

Rummaging through my desk, I found Matt's biography sheet for Dalton Williams, the retired navy man who'd hit his head on the bathtub. I circled the telephone number for Nora Bradshaw, the next door neighbor.

Chapter 38

The house, located in El Cajon, a suburb of San Diego, was actually a stucco duplex. I found it, despite Nora's vague directions, after making the commuter flight to San Diego again, this time renting a car from the economy counter. My credit card was getting a workout this month. I wasn't going to like the balance when the bill came in.

"You really were neighbors," I said when Nora Bradsaw indicated the door of the duplex next to hers as the colonel's place.

"We would've married, but I would'a lost my social security from my first husband. We couldn't afford it."

Nora was a petite woman with a pot belly. Liked her beer, I noted, seeing a can at her elbow.

"Course I might as well have. The colonel's social security was more than mine."

I nodded at her meaning. She would have been better off now.

"But I get by. I rent the other half out. Another gentleman. No trouble."

She eased herself into a La-Z-Boy and indicated for me to take the other recliner. The tiny living room boasted a huge television screen.

"We loved TV. He got that for us," she explained.

"We had a lot of fun. He never married, you know. He was an Indian."

"Really." People were full of surprises. "What kind?"

"That tribe in Idaho that wouldn't quite fightin'."

"Oh, yes. The Nez Perce." I recalled that shameful chapter of American history.

"He still got money from it. But he wasn't a reservation Indian. Didn't approve of it. Thought Indians should be Americans. That's why he was a career man."

"Was he really a colonel?"

"No," Nora laughed. "But he acted like it sometimes. He was an enlisted man for years, then worked his way up to petty officer."

"Did he know Jeffrey Randall when he was in the Navy?"

"Oh, yes. They go back for years. The colonel was like a father to Jeffie."

I shuddered to think that Randall could cold-bloodedly arrange the demise of a man who had treated him like a son.

"What happened the morning of the accident?"

"It could have happened in the night. We always slept in our own beds," Nora said virtuously.

"I went over late in the morning to take him some bran muffins I'd made. And there he was. Dead on the bathroom floor. Just like my first, Howard. He died in the bathroom, too." Nora seemed lost in pondering this curious coincidence.

"He'd hit his head?" I asked.

"His head was bashed in something awful. A shame, he was a good looking man."

"Was he a big man?" I speculated a large man might more easily come to grief in a bathroom accident.

"No. Slender. Graceful. Even at his age, could move like a cat. Said it was in his blood."

"How long had he been dead?"

"He didn't suffer, they said. Instant death. They couldn't pinpoint exactly the time of death. They can't, you know. Just approximate." She sounded sure of herself, an authority no doubt granted by watching whodunits on television.

"Why are you asking me all this?" Nora peered at me suspiciously.

"I believe the colonel's death may not have been an accident." I decided she could handle the truth.

"Really?" The woman's eyes lit up with excitement, as though this were one of her shows. Then reality set in and the light dimmed. "But then, who...?"

"We don't know." I thought I might be forgiven the slight allusion to being in an official capacity. "But we thought you could help out. Did you hear anyone or see anyone visiting Dalton, the colonel, the night before he died?"

"Let's see. That was his poker night. They met at his place. I heard 'em coming and going as usual."

"How many?" I dared to hope another lead lay just around the corner.

"Four sometimes five."

"Randall. Was he part of the group?"

"Not really. But sometimes he came and sat in, just for old times' sake. The colonel liked that."

"So he could have been there that night."

"He could of. I don't remember 'xactly."

I took note again of the beer can. Nora's mind might be a bit hazy on many events after the second or third beer. A defense attorney would shred her testimony to pieces even if she did remember more accurately.

"What about the other poker players?"

"It was just penny-ante." Nora was defensive.

I realized she'd granted me more authority than I'd intended. I hastened to reassure her. "Oh, I'm sure. We don't care about that."

"Well, you know, this was almost three years ago. Old guys like those, no telling where they've gone to."

"Then you never knew them?"

"No. I cooked stuff and took it over once in awhile. But I didn't pay much attention to them. Just old men playing poker and drinking beer." Nora sighed.

"You don't recall any of their names?"

"Don't think I ever paid any attention. They weren't my friends," she added sharply.

I was caught up short. I saw myself as I would have been had I not stopped drinking sixteen years ago. Nora's world was hazy and shrunken to the narrowness of television soaps and what kind of beer to buy. No normal curiosity. No caring about other people. No interest about world events other than how they might affect one directly.

But Nora surprised me. "I have a Navy yearbook of the colonel's. Maybe we can find out something from it."

She took a battered album from a shelf and handed it to me. Like a high school's there were photos and names of the officers and enlisted personnel aboard the carrier, U.S.S. Enterprise. It was dated 1951. I found Jeffrey Randall's name below a picture of a stern young officer in dress whites. The colonel, in the enlisted section, was a seaman in navy blue, serenely content in the midst of some hundred shipmates.

"He used to look at this book alot. Here are his poker buddies." She indicated the messages written so long ago in the margins by their portraits, in the brashness of the young.

I pulled a notebook out of my purse and wrote down their names. They might come in handy even if I didn't try to track them down now. Perhaps a diligent prosecutor would be glad to have them to establish Randall's opportunity.

I thanked Nora for her help and left. Despite the trip being just one more dead end, cumulatively I knew there were just too many indicators pointing to Jeffrey Randall. Sooner or later, I would have to get a break, something that was a definite connection.

The murder weapon! It flashed through my mind that Randall had to have hit the colonel over the head with something and that something was hard evidence. Randall had to dispose of it somewhere. Another lead for the prosecutor. In the meanwhile, perhaps Matt's investigator could find out something.

It was Barbara who pointed out later that that didn't fit Randall's profile.

"He'll set events in motion for an accident, or a poisoning, but he wouldn't actually wield a weapon."

"But what about the rifle?" I argued.

"He probably wouldn't hit a person directly. He'd

shoot out their tire so they'd crash."

I was impressed. "You should have been a shrink."

"It rubs off. Living with you." She smiled.

My heart was whole again. Despite the menace of Jeffrey Randall, my beloved believed in me again. How wonderful it was. She was telling me she agreed there was merit to my suspicions. She was telling me I wasn't crazy, obsessing on some scapegoat for life's imperfections. I was the one stuck with that lingering doubt.

Chapter 39

Two days later, a Thursday, Kathryn invited me to tour the new houses being built for the homeless by Shelterworks. I knew exactly what she was trying to do. Change my view of Jeffrey Randall as the diabolical cause of every accident and ailment known to humankind and replace it with that of a benign benefactor.

I agreed to go, not to be so easily converted, but as one more attempt to find some hard evidence, anything to connect Randall with his crimes.

Barbara declined the invitation, pleading the priority of another fact finding errand on her court case.

"What are you digging up, anyway?" I asked her.

"No much, so far. But there are some other wrongful terminations. Dolly says we'll have more of a case with as many as possible. A cumulative effect."

I could appreciate that. This was precisely the theory behind circumstantial evidence. It wasn't any one single thing. It was the weight of many items added up.

On the morning of Normand's accident, I hadn't paid attention to the houses themselves. Focus was an amazing thing. It could blind you to other elements in the picture.

The building sites were out on the east edge of town on some inexpensive land with drainage problems. Most house buyers were warned to stay away from this property. Too many problems with flooding.

"We've put in French drains. That won't be a problem, CC." Kathryn assured me. "And it's kept our unit price down, because the land was so cheap."

Abstract structures of ice cream sticks, all in the framing stage, nestled together like a fifties housing tract. A crew of men and women were together raising a framed wall under the contractor's direction. A winter sun glinted off metal brackets like a silver laser light show. For some reason, I liked construction sites. Security, perhaps. Warmth and shelter. The promise of safety. Despite Normand's accident.

"They build their own houses?" I caught on to the concept.

"Exactly. That way they'll have an investment in them. Pride of ownership."

"So, it won't be like an inner city housing project." I remembered how fast the housing developments on Divisadero in San Francisco had deteriorated to slums.

"Saves a lot of capital, too, I imagine."

"Absolutely." Kathryn warmed to the topic. "Each house is costing less than half what a private contractor would charge."

The sound of hammers was a syncopated beat, as walls were nailed in place. A supervisor danced around with a level, keeping the walls precise.

"That really is economical."

"And of course, we sell it to the client with no profit added, so it's affordable."

"No down payment?"

"Their labor is the down payment. Eight hours each week for the six months it's taking to build all houses," Kathryn explained.

I calculated that as being around one thousand dollars at minimum wage rates.

"But most of them are here every minute they're not at their regular jobs. These are the maids and waiters and store clerks. People who've been priced out of the housing market."

I was moved by Kathryn's faith in people to bootstrap themselves, if just given a chance at it. She was certainly deserving of her seat on the board.

"How does the financing work?"

"The land was donated. The materials were bought at cost in lots of ten. And the labor is all their own except the supervisor and the electrician who are on contract."

"How much from the agency then for each house?" I thought the subsidy would still have to be considerable.

"Not very much. I don't know the exact figures. I think around two thousand each for the electrician and the supervisor. And then administrative costs."

"How is Normand doing?" I remembered to ask.

"Better than could be expected. He's in the burn unit at Veteran's in Los Angeles. He's a brave fellow and his wife is plucky. They have Vera to help them out, too."

"Have they found out what went wrong?" I had to admit I could not see this accident related to Randall in anyway. It served him no purpose at all. Much the opposite, I should think.

"The investigation is still proceeding. Work is halted on that house." She indicated the first structure, looking completed from the outside. "They had to inspect all of the other sites, too, so it held us up a few weeks. But Jeffrey is handling everything very well. He's good in emergency situations."

"So how do they then purchase their homes?" I didn't want to hear anything good about Jeffrey Randall. Besides I knew how he didn't handle things so well the day of the accident. Tried to play detective, and then left the scene in a huff, then his display of insensitivity and uncaring about Normand. But there was no use in telling this to Kathryn. She wouldn't believe me.

"The clients buy their homes with mortgages just like you and me. If their credit is poor, which is often the case, the agency co-signs."

"Are there ever defaults?" My suspicious mind saw yet another income producing opportunity for Randall.

"I don't know about his operation in San Diego. I imagine some would default. Some of them are not very responsible," Kathryn conceded, looking a bit disappointed.

As usual I had gone too far.

"It is a wonderful concept," I hastened to assure her. "I wish self-help housing could be done everywhere."

"Housing industry wouldn't like it. Not big enough profits."

I was surprised again by Kathryn's astuteness. Our concept of elders is that they are sentimental and incapable of realistic perceptions. Also, I had to admit her ruse had worked. My confidence in Randall's ulterior motives was shaken. Shelterworks' self-help program seemed to be legitimate, functioning exactly as Kathryn said. There was a loose end, however. What about the people who didn't qualify for the building program? The real homeless, without jobs, without hope.

"How much does it take to feed and lodge the homeless?"

"I think the unit cost is ten dollars a day. An average stay is ninety days and we expect to serve about a hundred at a time at full capacity." Kathryn had the figures right off the top of her head.

"Ninety thousand a quarter," I calculated. That must be where Randall needed large suffusions of cash from the selling of seniors' homes.

"State and county funds kick in two thirds of that. Fundraisers and donations supply the rest and give us a reserve." Kathryn had anticipated my next question.

Chastened by what I had seen at the building sites, I was almost ready to throw in the towel. It was hard to find fault with something that was doing so much good for so many.

I looked again at the tidy stack of building materials, many sections already put together.

"You must get a discount on materials by buying them in quantity."

"Better than that. A lot of it is prefabbed out at Jeffrey's factory. Then hauled over here, ready to assemble."

"What? You mean Randall is the supplier?"

"Well, yes. A company he owns stock in. But that's why we can get the materials at deep discount."

I bit my tongue. Obviously, Kathryn did not see it was a conflict of interest. Nothing would dissuade her from seeing him as god-like. I toyed momentarily with leaking this to the papers and then decided against it. These people deserved their affordable housing. Who was I to meddle and ruin it for them?

The ever waiting chasm of depression threatened again to claim me, but, later that afternoon, a phone call from Matt perked things up.

Chapter 40

"We finally have the death certificates for the three so-called natural deaths. They are all signed by the same doctor."

"What was the cause of death?"

"Just stopped breathing in the night. Like a sudden infant death for seniors."

"You mean they are suspicious deaths?"

"Yes. Too much coincidence. Three women, all dying the same. It was over five years time, so no one in the police department or coroner's office thought anything of it. You know, different people handling different aspects of the cases. No reason to connect the three." Matt's voice was triumphant.

"Was there any sign of struggle?"

"No. Which eliminates the pillow over the face. But they all took medications."

"Can the investigator find out what any of those medications were?"

Overdosing was not out of the question. Or an adverse reaction from missing drugs in an already fragile system.

"We can try. But maybe it's time to turn this over to the police."

"Who was the doctor?" Matt shocked me with wanting to turn it over to the police, already. Somehow I thought we'd need more than that.

"Chester Widenmark. He's retired, though. And we don't know where he's gone. Vanished, it seems."

"What about his patient records? Don't they get turned over to whomever takes on his practice?" Certainly, therapists have to handle confidential files very carefully. Even destroying their contents after the requisite time elapsed.

"Not in this case. Apparently the files went with the doctor."

"What about neighbors of the ladies? Did they see anything, hear anything? Was Randall ever at their homes?"

"Yes, he often picked them all up and drove them places. A frequent visitor. But it means nothing by itself. I think the doctor is the lead for the police to open an investigation."

"All right." I wondered why I was dragging my feet. Here was our opportunity. We should seize it. Was I so obsessed with Randall, after all? Did my ego require that I single-handedly solve the case myself?

"By the way, Matt. Dalton Williams had a poker group that met every Thursday night. They might testify that Randall was at his house the night he died."

"Good. What were their names? I'll give them to the police, too."

I read off the old sailors' names to him, spelling them carefully.

"Is there anything else?"

"Charlotte Buchanan. Randall or Mildred probably spiked her drinks at a CARE dinner. The bar owner at the Jubilee, a women's place on Broadway, could testify that she drank cokes that night."

"Great! This is starting to come together."

We said goodbye and I hung up the telephone, wishing I could share his good feeling. The evidence was still flimsy. The doctor could very well have retired legitimately, taking confidential files for safekeeping.

I had to face the hard reality that what we had would never make a case. There were three 30-06 shells. One from the deer. One from my tire and the live one from Randall's cottage. But Blakely had resisted the idea of a ballistics test on Randall's rifle. Besides, if Randall was as smart as I suspected, he would have gotten rid of the rifle by now. And the poisoned bird seed.

We had five dead seniors in San Diego. The San Diego Five, I was coming to think of them. Two accidents, three natural causes.

He or Mildred had the opportunity to spike Charlotte's drink the night of her accident. And Randall was present the night of the colonel's accident. But so were a lot of other people.

The note of warning to Matt. His flu a possible poisoning, but again no proof.

Barbara's dismissal by the school board. Only the superintendent could connect her firing to Randall, and he'd closed ranks with the rest of the school board.

The poisoned birds. Maybe I could find something in the tool shed near his cottage. Something he might have overlooked. One tiny sunflower seed, perhaps.

There was still nothing that actually linked him to the deaths of the birds.

On the Call-a-ride accident, the sun had been in the east, but the van had faced west, turning south, putting it in the wrong position to blind the driver. Unless someone had helped out with a mirror. Definitely a possible linkage. His whereabouts for that time needed to be verified.

The marked obits for future soliciting of donations and/or board members. Nothing suspicious in itself, but put with the five deaths in San Diego and a disappeared doctor, it could be worthwhile as circumstantial evidence.

All possibilities, maybes, perhaps. Nothing conclusive. Unlike therapy, where the indicators, if enough of them, were often sufficient to proceed with a course of treatment. And whether true or not, believing helped make it so. A diagnosis, a treatment, a faith, and the patient got better.

But this situation just seemed to get worse. There was no diagnosis, no prognosis. The indicators weren't sufficient for a course of action. I wished I'd never gotten involved. Sinking into a morass of self pity as I was, I'd almost forgotten Kathryn. But of course. At least my pursuit of Randall had served to protect her, so far.

Chapter 41

The phone was ringing insistently. I fought my way up out of the bottom of a deep heavy sleep. The digital green glow said 2 a.m. That meant an emergency. My heart trip hammered as I grabbed the phone.

"It's Jennifer. I was arrested tonight at the protest. Only one phone call."

I could barely make out her words, because of background noise. It sounded like singing.

"Don't want Aunt Kathryn worried."

"Shall we come bail you out?" I didn't know what the protocol was.

Barbara lifted herself up onto an elbow looking first at the clock and then at me in disbelief. Whether for the hour or my willingness to bail someone out of jail, I didn't know.

"No, no, but thank you."

"Do you want an attorney?" I was confused. What did she want, anyway?

"We're trying to jam up the system. Refusing to bail out or get released on O.R. Want media to pay attention to us."

"Is it working?" The background commotion suggested a party rather than a jail.

"Well, I don't know. They've herded us all into the conservation corps camps. One telephone. Take turns. That's why I had to call you so late."

"How many of you are there?" I had to admit the dormant radical was being vicariously stirred by the principle of civil disobedience.

"Two hundred. But you know they'll claim a handful of radical lunatics. I need for you to explain to Auntie. Afraid if she hears it on the news tomorrow, could affect her heart."

"Don't worry. She'll be proud of you. We'll break it to her first thing tomorrow. She knew you were demonstrating."

I watched Barbara nod in comprehension and sink back into the warmth of the comforter.

The phone went dead. I held it for a moment to see if it was a momentary disconnect but at the incessant buzzing, hung up. They must have been limiting the time on their calls to a minute each.

Sleep did not return to me as I tossed and turned. I admired Jennifer for putting herself on the line to back up her beliefs, but loathed myself for not doing so. I could support their goals and contribute money, but I sure didn't put my person on the line.

Sleep eluded me with this painful settling of accounts with my conscience. Being older was no excuse, either. Fifty and sixty year olds could hold a picket sign and march just as well as thirty year olds.

It was then that what to do came to me. I got up. It was now 4 am. Barbara was sound asleep, her dark hair peeking out of the comforter. I took my pillow to the guest room. In the closet I located a sleeping bag and a fold-up cot. Then I hauled everything to the back terrace to set up a surveillance station. Tomorrow I would bring out the scopes and binoculars. I would keep watch on the neighborhood. Especially Kathryn's place. If it was my fate to take care of our own backyard, then I was going to do a damn sight better job of it. It was the only way to protect Kathryn and catch Jeffrey Randall red-handed.

The cot wasn't bad and the cold fresh air soothed me right back to sleep. A few hours later, day had dawned and I awoke to Barbara's disapproval.

"It's twenty-eight degrees out here at night."

"This bag is designed for twenty below." I was resolute. "Hot liquids before retiring and I'll stay snug as a bug."

"But what are you going to accomplish?"

"I'll hear if anyone is up there at night. Sound really carries off that hill. And I'll see them if it's during the day." She knew I was not to be persuaded otherwise.

Chapter 42

At my invitation, Blakely and Teresa came to look over the situation.

"We can let you have an extra radio. You can call either of us direct." Blakely approved of my surveillance set up, which he had suggested from the beginning.

"You're not to do anything else," Theresa warned. "If you hear or see anybody, you call us. I can be here in minutes."

"You're to act as a citizen's watch, only," Blakely emphasized.

"But I am an acting deputy." I pinned the badge to my wool shirt.

"Your bird watching skills make you a good observer," Blakely affirmed, grinning. "If it moves, it better be a bird."

Barbara shook her head, resigned to going into the house to get some coffee and bearclaws for our guests.

"Even if you're not out here twenty-four hours, just

watching as much of the time as you can will help a lot." Theresa poured herself coffee and delved into the pastry.

"I suppose I could spell her from time to time," Barbara allowed.

At my eager expression, she amended, "But not at night. I sleep in my own bed at night."

"It probably isn't necessary at night," Blakely agreed. "He's never done it in the middle of the night. He consulted a notebook. "Usually late dusk, sometimes early morning."

"Five-thirty in the morning once," I recalled. "It was still dark, too."

Later in the day, Kathryn peered over the fence to survey the apparatus surrounding me.

"What in the world are you doing? Have you lost it, girl?"

"What I'm doing is classified." I'd searched for just the right word. "No one is allowed to know about it."

"Oh. The sniper. You're still after the sniper."

"If you can't keep this top secret, we'll have to move the surveillance station," I warned her.

"Don't worry so. I won't tell anyone. I promise." Kathryn seemed a bit hurt.

But I was afraid she might tell Randall and warn him off.

For the next few nights, I slept soundly on the terrace. It was like camping out. The stars were astonishing in their brilliance and numbers. I saw several fall off into the horizon, evoking a primitive thrill every time. Our familiar landscape was rendered into an alien territory by the glittering moonlight.

Occasionally, I was awakened by an owl flapping

overhead, an opossum prowling the compost pile, or a deer browsing the garden.

But it was so peaceful, I'd almost forgotten why it was that I was sleeping outdoors.

It was still dark when I awoke, though faint rays of sun brightened the eastern sky. I guessed it was around five. Something had awakened me. A heavy blanket of quiet lay over the land. Not even the birds were stirring yet.

The frigid air knifed into my chest as I breathed deeply, trying to stay calm.

Then I heard a rustling from up on the hill. A deer, perhaps, roaming through the grass. But the hair on the back of my neck prickled. I unzipped the sleeping bag and sat up. I reached for my Rocsports by the cot.

Chapter 43

The sound was getting fainter, moving away from me up the hill. In a way I was relieved, yet something compelled me to hurry with the laces in my shoes. I'd slept in sweats so was ready to go when I grabbed the big service flashlight next to the cot and stood up.

"What is it?" Barbara was at the back door. I should have known she would be keeping this vigil, too.

"I don't know. Better call Blakely and Theresa on the radio and then go over to check on Kathryn."

"Don't you dare go up there." Barbara disappeared.

I stepped off the terrace carefully, and moved stealthily toward the sound, taking cover in the darker shadows of rocks and trees. My navy sweats blended into the darkness perfectly. I had to stifle a giggle at the notion that I should have worn camo face paint like the National Guard kids on maneuvers at Camp Roberts. A slight hysteria, I analyzed.

My breath was coming harder as I climbed the hill, straining to catch sight of the intruder. *Perhaps it's only a deer. No, it must be Randall. This is what you've been waiting for, keeping your vigil, sleeping out on the terrace like a nut in the middle of winter. Now go for it.*

Another rustling in the grass was closer now. I froze. My heart pounded. I heard a metallic click. It was the bolt on a rifle.

"Stop right where you are." His voice shot down, commanding and menacing.

"I know what you're up to. You can't get away with it." I made my voice sure and strong even though I was gasping for air.

"Who says? Women like you think you're so damned smart." His hoarse whisper drifted around me.

"Living without men. Unnatural." His voice hissed. "But you're no different than other women.

Parasites. Blood suckers. It was your daddy who paid for your fancy degrees." Accumulated venom kept oozing out.

"It's men who pay for your fees so you can live so high and mighty." His voice was closer.

"Just like Kathryn. Living on beyond her years. Sucking off the labor of her husband. The men drop dead of heart attacks. The women live on."

His resentments were unending. I knew I was in danger but I was hypnotized by his unveiling.

"I can understand why it looks that way to you." The therapist was still functioning.

"How can you? You're not a man or a woman." His voice was full of hate.

"Perhaps that's why I can understand it. I'm not caught up in either one."

"Don't give me your clinical techniques. It's too late for that. I have to get rid of you. You know too much."

"Then you did kill them." My voice quavered.

"Just helped them along. But you will have to commit suicide up here. You were acting despondent. You had been sleeping outdoors. Everyone knows you've been strange lately." He seemed to be working it out.

The hair on my scalp prickled as I realized he had been watching me, too.

"Then you wanted me to come up here after you." I gasped.

"Yes, you were easy."

"You shot my tire out?"

"Of course."

"And poisoned the birds?" I could hear a siren scream in the distance. If only I could stall him.

"Enough of this chitchat." He rustled in the grass.

"You can't get away with it, Jeffrey. The sheriff is on the way. Barbara knows you're up here."

"I planned this better than that. My car is up over the hill. I don't have to come down. And no one else has seen me up here."

I could hear him draw ever closer. Maybe only fifteen feet away by now. It dawned on me that if he was going to try to make it look like suicide he would have to get very near me. Arms length, an AA expression for fellowship, I thought irrelevantly.

"And if they do, all the more reason to take you with me." His voice was cold now, but close, too close. I still couldn't see him.

Desperate, I turned on the powerful flashlight and aimed it in his direction.

A shot rang out, in a cracking echo. Scared, my hands shaking, I threw the flashlight as hard as I could, knowing it was no match for a gun. But I was rewarded with an annoyed grunt. I'd actually hit him.

I heard him running through the grass up the slope, away from me. And then a new sound, hoofsteps pounding from the top of the hill. I thought it was a deer.

Chapter 44

It was a confusing jumble of events all happening at once. I saw Jeffrey Randall silhouetted on the cross fence in the early morning light. A second shot rang out. Randall slumped over the fence, while a horse and rider came over the hill. It was Jasper. And below me came Blakely and Theresa with their revolvers drawn.

Dumbfounded, my legs gave out. I couldn't go a step further. I sat down on the ground by a huge boulder and tried to catch my breath. The two factions moved quickly to surround Jeffrey as the morning sun came up to spotlight the scene in an unholy glow.

I can never forget the grisly sight of Randall's body draped across the barbed wire.

"Are you all right?" Jasper was beside me. "I heard that shot from clear over the hill. I was just getting ready to go out and check on some calves."

"I'm okay. Just a bit shocked. You better go down and see to Kathryn."

He nodded and wheeled away on the little Appaloosa to tear down the hill.

I watched Blakely and Theresa examine the body, then apparently discuss and decide to leave Jeffrey on the fence for the coroner to see.

Barbara caught up with me beneath the rock. “Looks like you got your man.”

“Don’t make me laugh.” I was still having trouble breathing.

“Over did it, did you, old girl?” Barbara helped me up. “Let’s go home.” Her amazon face was white underneath its tan.

Blakely and Theresa came to the house after the coroner’s crew took away Randall’s body.

“You sure had his number.” Blakely was admiring.

“What actually killed him?” I still didn’t really know.

“His own gun. A .22.” He looked at me meaningfully. Yet another caliber of gun. Not the 30-06, at all. “He ran into the fence. The bullet entered below his chin and lodged in his frontal lobe. Coroner said death was instantaneous.”

“But you got him good with that flashlight, CC.” Theresa patted me on the arm. “Nice lump on his head. Probably disoriented him.”

“So what is it, officially?” I persisted.

“Death by misadventure. Hunting accident. There’s nothing to support anything else.” Blakely was firm.

“Even though he almost killed both Kathryn and me?”

“We don’t have any proof of that.” Blakely looked ashamed.

"Even though he admitted having something to do with the deaths of the San Diego seniors?" I was angry again.

"Did he actually confess to killing them?" He looked interested again.

"Not exactly. He said he'd helped them die." I saw his point.

"I'm sorry, CC. The sheriff is through with this case."

"Just be glad it's over, CC. You won't have to be obsessing over him anymore." Barbara sounded very relieved.

"How is Kathryn taking it?"

"Just fine. Jasper is still with her and Phyllis came over to check her out. She had an erratic heart beat for awhile."

"Understandably. So did I." I had to grin in sheer relief.

Chapter 45

I felt like a hypocrite attending the memorial service for Randall, but not to attend would have been conspicuous in our small community, raising questions and fomenting gossip we'd rather not have. It was a simple ceremony, with a Baptist preacher citing Randall's good works as enough to admit him to the pearly gates. I doubted this, but resolved not to speak ill of the dead.

Also, I must confess it was one last chance to gather any hard evidence of Jeffrey's crimes. Obsessions don't die easily.

Mildred was there, dabbing at discreet tears. She was actually grieving.

Afterwards, outside the church, she pressed a package into my hands. "These tapes will explain how he worked it in San Diego. In return, I expect not to be charged with anything. Nor my daughter."

"Are you kidding? Accessory to murder?" It was incredulous.

"Jeffrey didn't murder anyone." Mildred seemed genuinely aghast. "He only embezzled. You can't think that. Never had it in him to hurt anything. I admit he was a strange bird. He had a thing about deer. But I knew he didn't kill anyone."

"You don't know that for sure," I argued. "What do you think he was doing up on that hill?"

"I don't know. Sometimes I was afraid of him, though. Didn't mean he couldn't," she conceded.

"What about the poisoning of Matt?"

"I didn't poison him. I merely sent the note to scare him off when he came down with the flu."

"That was not too smart. It just made Matt more determined."

"I know. I feel horrible. I didn't realize Jeffrey would go so far." She burst into fresh tears and fled the sun drenched church steps.

Somehow I believed her, even though I didn't want to.

Kathryn joined me. "It was a lovely service. I liked the part about good works for the right reasons."

I was amazed, realizing then that she had heard what she wanted to hear, as we are all wont to do more often than not. The truth was not acceptable in this case.

Vera came over. "Thanks for supporting my candidacy for the director's job."

"Oh, you'll do a great job." Kathryn patted her arm.

I caught from the corner of my eye an unlikely huddle of the school superintendent, Dolly Han and Barbara.

"Looks like an out of court settlement." I was happy now.

"Have you met Jeffrey's mother?" Vera asked.

I shook my head, looking around for the distinguished looking literary lady and finding her gone already.

"She donated Jeffrey's building supply company to Shelterworks."

"That's great." I could see how she'd have no interest in it, however.

"Now we can provide jobs, too." Vera's face was lit-up.

"Just a full service outfit," I grinned back. This was one strange funeral. Randall's good works were more apparent by his demise than his living.

"Did I tell you that Guy is going to serve as a consultant to our new AIDS support program?"

"Is that right?" I was impressed.

"The community needs it," Vera simply said.

"How is Normand doing, by the way?"

"Better than we could have hoped. He's mending very quickly and won't be needing any more skin grafts. In fact, he's agreed to be our new general manager on the building program."

"With construction safety classes?" I could have bit my tongue the minute this was out.

"Well, yes. That was Normand's proposal. How did you know?" Vera stared at me.

"Seems like a good idea," I mumbled.

"The investigation proved the accident was not Normand's fault." Vera was standing by her friend. "The team recommended steps for doublechecking all the work to ensure everyone's safety. Normand proposed going even further, to conduct safety classes to prevent mistakes."

I grinned and nodded, then remembered a loose end.

"By the way, did you check that address out by the Mushroom Farm?"

"Yes, it was one of our board members. A widow in her late seventies who started that farm with her husband."

I nodded, satisfied.

"We searched Randall's place." Theresa, out of uniform in a pretty dress, joined us. I was as surprised to see her at the service as I was to hear of the search. A warrant had been denied.

"It's a social occasion," she explained herself. "Funerals are the only times everyone in town turns out."

"What did you find?" I squirmed in embarrassment. I should have known going to funerals was a small town custom.

"No other rifle and no 30-06 shells."

"Well, obviously he got rid of them."

"Probably at the bottom of the lake." Theresa was smiling and greeting her neighbors.

"What?"

"The bottom of the lake. That's where everyone dumps things they want to get rid of."

"You could drag it?" I inquired hopefully.

"I'm sorry, CC. The sheriff has closed this case. It was only because we believed you that we investigated on our own time."

"I appreciate what you did." I suspected they had both risked their jobs. But it was hard to give up completely.

"No poisoned birdseed, either?"

"None. Probably in the lake, too."

I had the feeling there was evidence for a lot of crime in that lake. I would never look at it the same again.

Matt was at my elbow next. "What do you think?"

"It's confusing. I just don't know anymore."

I gave him the tapes from Mildred.

"Here's the proof of embezzlement, but I don't know about murder."

"We can't find the doctor." Matt frowned.

I could tell he didn't want to quit yet.

"You've got enough to explain the financial picture and change the expectations of your board." I was contenting myself with small victories now. I wasn't so sure of anything, anymore. Perhaps I was letting go of my obsession with him. Perhaps it was the after image on my retina, one I knew would always be there, of Jeffrey Randall in his green jacket, draped over the barbed wire.

Chapter 46

"But were the San Diego seniors actually murdered, or not?" Barbara wanted to know that evening as we shared a cup of tea after the news broadcast.

"I'm not sure anymore. I know he acted in some way to contribute to their deaths. He admitted that. The important thing is that he did obviously mean some harm to Kathryn."

"And to you." Barb's eyes got big again. Her affirmation was delicious.

"And to the lady out at the Mushroom Farm?"

"Yes. He used the ruse of taking pictures to scope places out."

"And you stopped that very nicely." Barb's voice quavered, but she sounded proud of me.

Neither of us would forget my close call up on the hill for a long time.

"What could be debated, endlessly, is whether I had a hand in helping to make things happen." I was continuing to give this notion a great deal of thought.

Chapter 47

I thought that was the end of the entire matter of Jeffrey Randall but a few weeks later Matt Sorens called.

"We've found the doctor. He's confessed that Randall paid him to administer overdoses to the three seniors." His voice on the telephone was full of triumph.

"Who found him?"

"The San Diego police. They didn't give up."

"Where was he?"

"Not far away at all. In Palm Springs under a new identity. Broke down and confessed the minute he was apprehended."

"Must have been on his conscience." I could well imagine how the deaths might have haunted him.

"He knew nothing about the two accidents, but the police had enough circumstantial evidence, thanks to you, to tie it all to Randall."

"You have yourself to thank, Matt. It hasn't been an easy way to make a career comeback."

But I must confess to a surge of satisfaction, something I rarely allowed myself, knowing all too well the penalty for excessive pride as well as the price of not minding my own business.

"No, but the board now understands funding a nonprofit agency is not easy. They are working harder, too. We will rebuild CARE together."

A thrill of pride ran up my spine. "Nice going, Matt."

"Isn't it a curious coincidence, though, that Randall's father died accidentally and here he was killing off seniors and making them look like accidents?"

I had thought about this also. "Perhaps there are no coincidences."

"What do you mean?" Matt sounded interested.

"The theory is that we repeat our family of origin patterns until the issues are resolved. It's a way of trying to fix what happened to us as children."

It was then that I heard myself admitting I was still trying to repair my depressed father by taking on Jeffrey Randall in the first place.

Perhaps I *had* played a part in making these events happen. And in this admission came a subtle release.

Coming Soon

from Clothespin Fever Press

A NEW
Cynthia Chenery Scott suspense novel

MONEY seems to bring out the worst in people. It may not be the root of all evil, but illegally gotten money, especially, can cause folks a great deal of trouble. And trouble seems to follow me around quite a lot. Not that I look for it. But crises just seem to fall in my lap. I also have difficulty minding my own business, which probably accounts for why I became a therapist to begin with, a line of work that thrives on trouble.

Dirty Money by Pele Plante

Put yourself on our mailing list. Write:

Clothespin Fever Press
5529 N. Figueroa St.
Los Angeles, CA 90042